# HEART BREAKING

## BEST SERVED COLD
### BOOK 3

## MAGGIE ALABASTER

# TRIGGER WARNINGS

Murder

CNC

Degradation

Domination

Spanking

Drugging

Kidnapping

Car related violence

Mentions of child SA (vague)

# CHAPTER 1
## HARLOW

"Angel's Redemption. I like it." Boner looked up at the sign above the door.

The typography matched my other restaurant, Angel's Rest, but this sign was surrounded by flowers and balloons, ready for opening night.

He put an arm around my shoulders and pulled me to him.

"Ready as I'll ever be." It took six months of hard work and late nights to get here. The renovation of the late Solomon Danforth's restaurant was extensive, but done with care and thought. Now, it was more my style, but the changes didn't mess with the previous ambiance.

"Don't look so down, love," Boner leaned over to

kiss my temple. "This is gonna go gangbusters, just like Angel's Rest."

"I know," I said softly.

"Feeling restless?" he guessed. "Me too. It's been a while since I've…let off some steam."

I didn't have to ask what he was referring to. We'd been busy with the restaurant and hunting down the last two men on my list. Here and there we found predators like them, but Hypnos and Zeus seemed to have gone underground after Danforth and Granger Fairfield's deaths. As if they thought someone might be coming after them.

Okay, they were right. Someone was. Several some-ones. I loved my job as chef and restauranteur, but my life's work was to rid the world of predators who preyed on innocent people, especially young people.

There was a special place in hell for all of them, and I was happy to deliver them there.

"That's one of the reasons I'm here," he added. "I thought maybe after opening night we could go on a little playdate."

"Oh?" I asked, tilting my chin up to look into his blue eyes.

"Trust me," he said easily, "you're going to love it."

"I do trust you," I told him.

We almost died together six months ago. A thing

like that brought people closer together. Besides, Edward 'Boner,' Bonegard, was an easy man to trust. I'd come to love him deeply. He was good at reading people and keeping my spirits up when the world got dark. Darker than usual.

"I trust you too," he said. "Now, do I get a guided tour of the new pub?"

I nudged him in the side with my elbow. "This is *not* a pub."

He grinned, amused he got a rise out of me. "Of course it's not," he said narrowly, dodging another jab from my elbow. "It's a fancy arse place, if you ask me."

"It should be, for the price."

After we killed Solomon Danforth and left his remains in the restaurant, the price was lower than it might have been. Still, it was eye-watering and a risk. Taking over even a successful restaurant wasn't without its potential pitfalls. Especially when I gave the restaurant menu a facelift. I kept some of the classics on there, customer favorites, but added a few of my own.

Especially my famous meatballs.

"You'll make all of that back in the first week," he predicted.

I gave him the side eye. "We'd be lucky to make it

back in the first *year*. But I appreciate the vote of confidence."

"Any time." He brushed his lips over mine, before grabbing my hand and pulling me toward the door. Laughing, I followed him inside.

The smell of new paint tickled my nose, but I had to admit it looked good in here.

The floors were polished to a brilliant shine. All of the tables and chairs were new. The walls were decorated with mythical imagery, painted by a local artist. Angels. Seraphs. A unicorn and dragon here or there.

My particular favourite was an angel standing in the centre of one wall, her wings spread, golden and glowing. Her face was tilted up toward the ceiling, like she was thanking the universe for her existence.

"Be careful, love," Boner said. "I might come in here with a saw and cut that out so I can put it in my gallery."

I rolled my eyes at him playfully. We both knew he wouldn't do that, but he appreciated good art when he saw it. This was definitely it.

"How are you going for staff?" he asked carefully.

"I decided to keep most of them," I said. "Cass ran a thorough check on all of them, and they came up clean. And I know you followed most of them." I arched an eyebrow at him.

He responded with an innocent look, as if beer wouldn't evaporate in his mouth.

"Are you accusing me of stalking?" he asked, pretending to be affronted.

"If he looks like a stalker and acts like a stalker, then he's probably a stalker?" I suggested.

He placed a hand over his heart, leaning back as though I stabbed him there.

"I'm hurt," he said, trying to hold back a smile but failing. "It's not stalking. It's… being careful. Making sure the people you're working with aren't going to betray you."

He didn't add 'again.' We both remembered what Gina did, working with Solomon Danforth against us. Murdering Erin, who was doing nothing more than trying to live her best life and make something of herself. If Gina wasn't dead, she'd be in my torture box, waiting to die slowly. Could I have kept her alive for six months? I might have tried. For what she did, there was no forgiveness. No redemption.

I sure as hell didn't name the restaurant after her. No, I named it after myself. I wanted redemption for not seeing what Gina was doing. If I'd known, I might have been able to stop her from killing Erin.

Besides, Angel's Rest and Angel's Redemption worked as brand names. Ironic, because I was no angel. Not really. I did the best I could for other people, but I'd done some nightmarish things as well.

Like putting human flesh in my meatballs. Only the bad guys that deserved it. Call me judge, jury, executioner and disposer of assholes.

"I appreciate you," I told him.

I made my way through the eating area, toward the kitchen. It hadn't needed a makeover, just a refresh, a bit of paint here, new utensils, a few new pots. Nothing major. Just enough to make the kitchen the way I wanted it.

"Where the magic happens," Boner said, leaning against the doorframe.

"Good morning, Chef." A couple of my new staff were already at work preparing for lunch.

"Kayla, Dave." I gave them both a nod. Kayla was going to be head chef here, and Dave, her sous chef. I'd still be working at Angel's Rest, but checking in here every day to make sure everything was running smoothly.

I thought about giving myself the job of head chef here, but I was comfortable at my other restaurant. That place was home. This? This was an asset.

Besides, Cass was working for me now over at Angel's Rest, washing dishes and learning how to cook, while also handling a lot of my admin. When it came to computers, he was better at all of that than I was. Which wasn't saying much, to be honest. Technology and I had a pretty good relationship, but I preferred to be in the kitchen, preparing meals and coming up with new recipes. I wanted to be Chef Stabby, not Chef Tech. I'd leave that to him.

"I've…" Jules Titmus stopped in the doorway. "There you are. I just came to say I gave the electrical box an overhaul. The wiring in this place was a fucking nightmare."

He glared at me like I was responsible for putting the wires there in the first place. Of course he did. Jules and I had a tense relationship at best. Cass' brother was the epitome of grumpy. Fortunately, Boner's sunshine and Cass' golden retriever personality balanced it out.

"Thank you," I told him sincerely. "I appreciate you taking a look."

"Lucky I did or this place would have burnt down." His gaze slid to Boner.

If I didn't know better, I think he was accusing the Englishman of something. Maybe the intention of lighting a match in here.

If you hadn't realized by now, Jules had a chip on his shoulder the size of Manhattan.

"You're a regular lifesaver," Boner said with a hint of sarcasm. "Now I know what to get you for Christmas: a cape."

Jules flipped him off, while Boner grinned.

"You're coming back for dinner, aren't you?" I asked, posing the question to Jules. "I had a table set aside for you, Cass, Boner, and Archer."

Archer Hardwick was the fourth of the guys in my crew. A playwright who was obsessed with the internet and all manner of information found on there. Useful or otherwise. He was always ready with interesting facts or bizarre observations, always delivered with a straight face.

"I'll be here," Jules said, with a hint of reluctance. "Cassius insisted." Of course Cass had. When he was determined, he knew how to get his way. It was one of the things I liked the best about him. One of many, if I'm honest.

"Me too," Boner said. "I can't wait to see what's on the menu tonight."

I gave him a warning look. If I was going to use any 'meat' I sourced myself, it was going to be served at Angel's Rest, not here. Kayla and Dave were inno- cent. I wanted to keep it that way. I had enough accessories to murder without adding them to the list.

"It's going to be amazing," I said, giving Kayla a smile. She'd worked for another restaurant in the city before I hired her to work here, an establishment where she never would have been promoted or her skills recognized.

If there was anything I hated, it was unrecognized and unappreciated talent. With her in the kitchen, the place was going to thrive. And so was she.

Dave was one of the original staff, but he also wasn't given much responsibility until now.

He'd shown me what he could do, and I gave him the chance. I knew he'd take it and run with it. People usually did when you let them.

"No pressure," Kayla said with a laugh. Her eyes widened as if she was intimidated, but I knew she was up to this, and so did she.

It didn't hurt to have a bit of humility though. I'd met plenty of arrogant chefs. I didn't want one working for me. I sure as hell didn't want to become one. Yelling at my staff and belittling them. That wasn't the way to get the best out of people. No, I preferred to respect the people I worked with. They gave it back, most of the time.

Like always, the memory of Gina rubbed hard against my mind. Anger, disappointment, and wariness haunted me every time I thought about her.

I liked Kayla and Dave, but I was going to be keeping a close eye on them. If either of them was working with the enemy behind my back, they'd be on the menu.

"I need to get back to Angel's Rest to get lunch sorted," I said reluctantly.

That restaurant would be closed for dinner so I could be here tonight, but I had reservations for a handful of customers. Some sort of corporate work lunch they wanted me to cater.

I hoped like hell I hadn't bitten off more than I could chew, trying to run two restaurants. At some point, I'd have to trust someone to take over the kitchen at Angel's Rest, but not today. Today I wanted to cook to get my mind off tonight's grand opening. There was always a chance no one would turn up, in spite of all the bookings. It would suck if, after all the work we'd put in, I fell on my face.

I didn't want to do that to my staff. They were all relying on me for their wages, their livelihoods.

"It's going to rock," Boner told me. My thoughts must have been written all over my face.

"I hope so," I whispered.

If it didn't, we could let off steam afterward.

# CHAPTER 2

## HARLOW

"Hey," Cass greeted as I stepped through the door into the office. His brow creased.

"What is it?" I asked, looking down at the laptop open in front of him.

"I was looking into Hans Getzoff," he said. His eyes flicked toward the screen.

"The detective who's looking into the death of Solomon Danforth and Granger Fairfield. What did you find?"

"Nothing new," he said with a shrug.

"But?" I prompted.

Reluctantly he continued, "They seem to have connected a few deaths with one killer. Some guy named Carl disappeared around the same time as

Fairfield. Apparently he was into all sorts of shady shit, but they couldn't prove it."

I nodded slowly. I was well acquainted with Carl. Boner and I dispatched him together.

"I was thinking," he said, sitting back and pushing his hair off his forehead. "Should we send them some information?"

I tossed my bag down on the desk.

"What, like my name and address?" I knew he hadn't meant that, but I couldn't resist teasing him.

"I would never..." He started to say before he realized. I'd baited him and he'd taken it hook, line and proverbial sinker.

"I meant information about these... *People.*" His voice was tight.

The people we were after had taken his younger brother from him. Augustus Titmus was the youngest of three after Jules and Cass. He took his own life after Granger Fairfield abused him.

Pain still lingered in Cass' eyes when he thought about Auggie. Chances were it always would, the same way mine undoubtedly looked when I thought about my sister, Lottie. She was also abused and murdered by these men.

Most, I hunted down and killed. Two remained, men who called themselves Hypnos and Zeus.

Fancy names for pieces of shit.

Once I found out who they were, they'd be dead. After I gave them the chance to experience the kind of suffering she'd gone through before she died.

I put a hand on his shoulder and squeezed lightly.

"I've tried," I told him. "Early on I sent information about what happened to my sister and they did nothing. If she was rich, powerful and male, maybe then…"

That's what these men were: rich and powerful. They thought they were invincible. Untouchable. The police wouldn't dare to go after them. So I had to.

Ironically, the police wouldn't hesitate to come after me for doing it. Who said there was no justice in this world? Sometimes it seemed there wasn't, not unless you went out and found it yourself. It wasn't for nothing Boner jokingly referred to us as Vigilante University. The name was fitting.

"Getzoff might be more receptive," Cass said. He didn't look convinced.

"I'd still like to know why he turned up at Boner's gallery that night," I said thoughtfully.

"He might have been on to Solomon Danforth," Cass suggested.

"I prefer that explanation than thinking he had an inkling to what I was up to," I said. "He might have been about to arrest Solomon, but we got to him first."

Technically, he got to us, pinning us down in Archer's apartment. We got the last laugh there. He and Gina got the last breath.

"Would it hurt to send him some information and see if he acts on it?" Cass said.

"What information do we have?" I asked. Nothing, as far as I knew, we hadn't acted on ourselves up until now. "Boner said he had someone he wanted to deal with tonight." I rubbed my temples thoughtfully.

Cass swallowed hard. He'd seen the things I did and he'd still stuck around, mostly observing rather than taking part. He was getting used to the bloodshed, but his stomach wasn't up to it the way mine was. Maybe I was more cold-hearted than him.

"If we tell Getzoff anything, we can't go after them," I reasoned. "It might be the thing he's waiting for. We tell him where to go and he uses it to pin us down. Either tracking the information back to us or waiting for us to act and catching us red-handed. Literally."

"What do we do then?" Cass asked. "If this guy comes after you…"

"I can deal with a cop," I assured him.

During the brief conversation at the gallery party, he'd given me no indication he knew who I was. Not what I did in my spare time anyway. There was no suspicion in his gaze. No attempt to follow me or ask me questions.

He seemed like nothing more than a guy who thought I was the right person to hit on. Or a distraction while he was waiting for Solomon to make a misstep.

Getzoff was either clueless or a really good actor. I won't lie, the latter was slightly terrifying.

"You're not going to…" Cass adjusted his glasses and winced, his gaze toward the kitchen.

"I'll do whatever I have to do to keep us safe," I told him. If that meant making Hans Getzoff into spaghetti Bolognese, so be it.

Hopefully it wouldn't come to that. I didn't like messing with the police, not unless they were corrupt. As far as I could tell, this guy was just doing his job. Trying to keep the public safe from harm. I wanted the same thing, we just came at it from different angles. Mine slightly less legal than his. A lot messier too, most likely. Although, mine resulted in less paperwork.

"So we don't tell him anything," Cass said, slowly closing the laptop.

"I don't know what we'd tell him anyway," I admitted. "Boner didn't give me any details."

"If this is something we can't deal with, we'll try to find a way to let Getzoff know."

"Then we'll watch him," Cass said, pushing himself up from his chair and wrapping his arms around me.

"Definitely," I pressed my mouth to his, tasting the chocolate milkshake he must have just finished. "If he goes after them, we'll know he's doing the right thing. If not…"

Cass nodded slowly before leaning in to press his face into my red hair.

"You always smell so good," he whispered.

"Not always," I said with a small laugh.

Sometimes I smelled like death.

"Always," Cass insisted. "You smell like lavender and…something else." He sniffed. "I don't know, but it smells amazing." He nibbled on my earlobe, making me shiver.

"It might be garlic," I told him. I cooked with so much of it, I should buy shares in a garlic farm.

That might be my retirement plan. Move to the country and grow the bulb. Maybe have some pigs. They were good at disposing of unwanted meat, amongst other things.

"It's not garlic, but I can smell that too," Cass said.

"Of course you can, it wouldn't be an Italian restaurant if there wasn't garlic."

He laughed softly, his chest vibrating against mine.

"I suppose it wouldn't," he agreed.

"We should get to work," I said reluctantly. I'd happily let him sidetrack me, with an orgasm or two, but we had lunch to prepare for.

I should have closed Angel's Rest today too. Kayla might need me over at the other restaurant. Or I could be over there obsessing about tiny details. Did we have enough forks?

We had enough forks.

I took care of that a month ago. Maybe longer. Spoons then? No, we had enough of those too.

Everything over there was going to be fine. I knew that. A little bit of faith in myself wouldn't go astray at the best of times. On a day like today, I was justified in being a little nervous.

I took his hand and we walked together to the kitchen. We pulled out all the pots and pans we needed and started to prepare everything.

"I like working for you," he said, slicing quickly through a pile of tomatoes.

"Because it smells nice?" I teased.

He grinned. "That doesn't hurt. But I like being here with you and I like learning new things. You know what they say. If you stop learning, you might as well…"

He trailed off. We both knew he was about to say, 'die.'

"Right," I said quickly. "It's good to keep the brain active and fresh. And keep challenging ourselves." I frowned. "I sound like a motivational quote. Archer would be proud."

Cass laughed and tipped the cutting board up to slide the pieces of tomato into the pot. "Yeah, he would," he said. "But he always is."

I glanced over to him as a blush crept up his cheeks.

"He is or you are?" I asked knowingly.

He scraped the last of the seeds off the board. "Both. We're both proud of you and we both love you."

"I love you both too," I said as I finished browning the meat for the Bolognese sauce. And started to add the herbs he'd already sliced for me.

"I'm lucky I met you. All of you."

Even Jules, although I still didn't know where he fit in the equation. We'd been at each other's throats since we met. Neither of us had let up. Sometimes we'd call an uneasy truce, but in the next minute one of us was snarking at the other. Trying to bait each other and get the last word. Was that how we were always going to be? Probably, but it did complicate the situation. On the other hand, it made it interesting.

Sparring with someone who wasn't trying to kill

me was entertaining. And when it came down to it, neither of us meant the other any harm.

Mostly.

"I'm the lucky one," Cass said.

"Oh yeah?" I asked him over my shoulder. "How do you figure?"

He put down the board and knife and stepped over to me, chest pressed against my back.

"Because I get to listen to you come," he whispered in my ear. "When lunch service is over, that's what's going to happen."

Gone was the golden retriever persona, replaced for a moment by his dominant side.

My heart raced. "Are you trying to make me wet through the whole lunch service?" I asked.

"That's exactly what I'm doing." He kissed my hair and stepped away to clean the board.

I took a breath to clear my head. Vaguely aware of the back door opening and my servers stepping inside. Shelly and Yvette. Both started working for me shortly after Gina and Erin died. Both were professional and efficient. Both had a difficult few years, living both in shelters and on the streets. These were exactly the kind of women I killed for. Exactly the kind of people I wanted to help.

Giving them a job was the start they needed to get their lives back on track. Like Kayla and Dave, they'd been thoroughly vetted and watched for signs of an ulterior motive. If any was found, they wouldn't be working here.

So far, they were clean, but I hadn't been able to bring myself to trust them the way I did my previous staff. Once bitten and all that.

Honestly, after the things they'd been through in their lives, that went both ways. I also had to earn their trust.

There was a big difference between being someone's boss and being their friend. That was a bridge we hadn't worked our way across yet. Would we? I hoped so.

I wanted to surround myself with people I could trust, who trusted me. For people like us, that was huge. More than I deserved, maybe, but still something I'd work toward.

I gave them both a smile in greeting and went back to preparing the sauce and starting on the pasta. At the same time, trying to ignore the way my clit throbbed. One I knew he had every intention of keeping.

This was going to be a long lunch service.

# CHAPTER 3
## HARLOW

I just finished plating up the last bowl of spaghetti when a shadow appeared in the the corner of my eye. Holding back a flinch, I glanced up to see Archer in the doorway, his appreciative gaze on me.

I won't lie, his expression was good for my ego, considering my hair was a mess and I was wearing my chef jacket. The look he gave me, I could have been wearing lingerie or a ball gown, with heels.

I flashed him a quick smile, cleaned the droplets of sauce from the side of the bowl and handed it to Yvette, who took it and the other three over to the table.

"What are you doing here?" I asked as I leaned over to wash my hands in the sink.

"I thought I'd help you clean up from lunch," he

said. "You know what they say, many hands make for light work."

"They do say that," I agreed. "It's thoughtful of you to come and help out. I'd really like to get out of here and over to Redemption."

He glanced around the kitchen. Nodded at Cass before returning his gaze to me.

"What can I do?"

That was a good question. I kept a tight ship here. As much as possible, we cleaned up the mess as we went, but there were always things to be done at the end of a shift. Today was no exception.

"It's not glamorous, but if you can take the trash out to the dumpster, I'd appreciate it."

I jerked my head towards the can in the corner, the bag spilling over the rim.

"Consider it done." He carefully tied the neck and carried it out.

I handed the last of the pots to Cass to rinse out before they went in the dishwasher and grabbed up a cloth to wipe around the stove.

"Is Archer looking for a job here too?" Cass asked jokingly.

"Archer has a job," Archer said, stepping back into the kitchen. "I'm working on a play right now. It's about a chef."

"It's not about Chef Stabby, is it?"

I didn't want to be the next big thing on Broadway. The demon chef who murdered people and turned them into dinner. For one thing, it wasn't original, as musicals went. Although maybe there was more room on the stage for something other than the Demon Barber of Fleet Street. The man who sliced his customers throats instead of shaving them. While singing, if the musical was to be believed.

"If it is, can I be in it?" Cass asked eagerly.

"You could be the cute nerdy guy who does the washing up," I told him.

"You think I'm cute?"

"Of course I do. I think you're both cute," I told them.

I cocked my head at Archer. "You didn't answer the question." If he thought I was going to let that slide, he'd have to think again.

"It's not about Chef Stabby." He placed another bag in the trash can and smoothing down the sides. "It's about a chef who helps people in need. People who've had a hard life. Bad things happened to them." He pressed his lips together.

"I could still be the cute nerd that does the washing up," Cass pointed out.

Archer regarded him. "Possibly. I have to finish it first."

My face heated. "You're writing a play about me?"

"It's worthy subject matter," Archer said with a twitch of his shoulder. "And it'll draw attention to the fact there are people out there who have real need. I want to get it in front of as many rich and famous people as I can." The look in his eyes suggested he might tie them down if they didn't turn up to watch voluntarily.

"Archer Hardwick, social justice warrior," I said, approvingly.

"What's the point of art and literature if you can't use it to speak for you?" Archer said. "It's all political at the end of the day."

"I suppose it is," I agreed. His angle certainly was. If he wrote a play about Chef Stabby trying to level the playing field for innocent people, that was too.

"No one would believe the other story," Archer said, opening the dishwasher for Cass to load the pots inside.

"I hope not," I said. "It'd be hard to keep a low profile if—"

I stopped talking when Shelly stepped into the kitchen with a pile of plates and bowls in her arms. Cass took them from her and she hurried back out.

"We shouldn't be talking about this stuff here," I said.

Not while Shelly and Yvette were around anyway. The last thing I needed was for them to stumble on what their boss and her boyfriends were really like. That would be awkward to say the least, and dangerous at worst.

They could go to Detective Getzoff and tell him what they knew. Or I'd have to stop them from doing that, which was the last thing I wanted.

No, the less they knew, the better.

If you told me a few months ago, even four other people knew what I was doing, I'd shoot down the idea. Before that, I largely worked alone, only sharing the occasional kill with Archer. It seemed easier that way. Safer. The fewer people who knew what you were up to, the less chance there was of being found out and turned over to the police.

Or people like Hypnos and Zeus.

Now though? I couldn't imagine doing this without my men. Having someone to talk about this stuff with, was keeping me sane. I knew the value of that as a serial killer. Sanity was fragile. Something easily taken from us if we let all of this get to us. We'd escalate and do something stupid. Go on a killing spree or expose ourselves in some way.

No, I had to hold onto my sanity with everything I had.

Archer placed his hands on my shoulders and turned me around so he could massage the tension out of them.

"You're doing a good thing," he said. "The percentage of people who see wrongdoing in the world and actually act on it is smaller than it should be. If they see other people doing the right thing, they're much more likely to do it too. There are whole chapters in psychology textbooks about it."

"I wish I could say I'm surprised," I said, dropping my chin to give him better access. "I've seen it firsthand. If a man is harassing a woman, people will watch or pretend they can't see until finally someone steps in. Then they'll do it too."

"You're one of the people who always steps in," Archer said. "You don't hesitate."

"So are you," I reminded him. "I've never seen you hold back when someone needed help."

"Yes, but the things I do aren't suitable for public consumption," he said in my ear. "So I resort to writing about it instead."

"We all do our part," I told him. "All of us are doing what we can."

"Sometimes it doesn't feel like it's enough." He exhaled softly, his breath soft and warm on my neck.

"I know what you mean," I said. "Sometimes it feels like for everyone we deal with, there's three or four or ten more still doing it." That was probably a conservative estimate.

"I wish that side of our lives paid better. Then we could do it full-time," he said, as dry as ever.

I choked back a laugh. "That would be living the dream, wouldn't it?"

Full-time serial killer had an interesting ring to it. Who would pay us? People were professional assassins, so I supposed there was a market for it.

Unfortunately, in our case, the people who were the most likely to pay for our services were also the people we were dealing with. People with power and influence. People who'd pay an assassin to take us out if they knew where to find us.

Cops, I could deal with. A professional assassin was another thing. Part of me was curious how I'd measure up again them. Mostly, I didn't want to know. I suspected I wouldn't come out of it alive. Maybe I wasn't giving myself enough credit. It was possible I'd take them down with me. I'd give it a good try. I hadn't given up anything without a fight yet. I wasn't going to start any time soon.

"Until then, I better keep on cooking." I looked out into the seating area, as Yvette and Shelly packed up the last of the dishes. The remaining customers made their way out the door.

They seemed to have enjoyed their lunch. They tipped well. Of course they did. I made sure the food and service here was impeccable.

Hopefully Archer would remember that when he was writing his play.

"Have a great night," I said as they grabbed their things to head out the door.

"Thanks, Chef," Yvette called over her shoulder.

She reminded me too much of Erin. So much so, I kept my distance from her, making sure to be professional and not too friendly. Gina used Erin against me. I didn't want anyone doing the same to either of these women.

Cass stacked the last of the crockery into the dishwasher, turned it on and turned around.

"I made you a promise," he said, his eyes dark. "You're going to have at least one orgasm before we leave."

"I like that promise," Archer said approvingly.

"Of course you do. Listening to Harlow come is better than music." Cass laced his fingers and rested his hands in front of himself, over his cock.

"Archer, take her clothes off. Taste her pussy."

Archer didn't tend to jump when Cass told him to, not in the way Boner did, but he didn't hesitate to ease my chef jacket off my shoulders and place it aside before starting on the rest of my clothes.

I stepped out of my pants and my panties and let Archer lift me up and place me on the clean counter.

His eyes on me, he knelt down in front of me and parted my thighs with his hands.

"You smell like heaven," he whispered, all but burying his nose in my pussy. He teased my clit with first the tip of his nose, then the tip of his tongue. Drawing my clit between his teeth and sucking gently.

I quivered at his touch, wanting more. After a few moments of me rolling my hips to try to find the exact place where I needed him, he looked at me with amusement in his eyes.

Of course he was doing it on purpose. He knew exactly where my clit was. He was teasing me, drawing out the moment before he dove back in and started to devour me.

I gave him a small eye roll, but then they were rolling into the back of my head instead as his tongue drove me higher and higher.

"Just like that," Cass said. "Harlow, touch your breasts."

My gaze shifted from Archer to him. I raised my hands and cupped my breasts. My palms made my nipples harden. The sensation added to my arousal.

"So fucking perfect," Cass whispered. "So fucking ours."

Archer murmured his agreement, the sound

coming from the back of his throat. At the same time, his lips smacked wet against me.

I couldn't hold back any longer. I arched my back, pressing my pussy hard against Archer's mouth as I came, riding his face and drawing out the pleasure for as long as I could.

The whole world melted away. Nothing left but heat and bliss. Release leaking from my pussy onto Archer's lips. His tongue working harder to keep me afloat before I finally sank back down to earth.

"I'll never get enough of watching that." Cass blinked a couple of times as if to clear his vision. He seemed to be as lost in the moment as I was. Getting off on my orgasm.

"We should—" I started. I wanted to return the favor. Right here, right now.

"Get ready for tonight," Cass finished for me as Archer pushed himself to his feet. "There's time for more later."

I wanted to feel them inside me, but he was right. I needed to go and get ready for the big opening. When that was done, we'd have a private party.

# CHAPTER 4
## ARCHER

tatistically speaking, one hundred percent of the time, Harlow took my breath away. Tonight, she sucked the air right out of my lungs, making it almost impossible to breathe.

I was the kind of animal that required oxygen for survival, so I forced myself to inhale and exhale. My eyes never left her.

She wore a backless gown that fell just above her feet. The amount of cleavage she had on display was minimal, but somehow hotter than if she was naked. Black heels made her even taller, and her legs longer than sin. Not that I believed in sin, as such. That is to say, it's a judgement people make. Me, not so much.

"I don't know why you take any weapons with you when you kill people," Boner said, leaning against the back of a chair. "I think I'm dead just looking at you."

His blue-eyed gaze drank her up the same way I was.

Boner's words were more elegant than Cass' response. He stood, gaping, like he'd never seen anyone or anything like her before.

She laughed. "I don't think I'll try it. I have a feeling it won't be effective on anyone but you three."

"Anyone with average eyesight would see how gorgeous you are," I said. "But if you tried to kill with how you look right now? It would be dangerous if they caught you on camera."

"You'd be easily recognizable," Cass agreed. Somehow he managed to oil the hinge in his jaw and get it closed again. Most of the way at least; he was still staring openly.

"You guys look incredible too." She swung her gaze from one of us to the other, taking in our dark suits and ties. Mine brightly colored, the other two more muted, like they didn't want to steal the limelight from her.

That was a first for Boner. He usually enjoyed being the center of attention. Tonight, though, was about Harlow and her new restaurant.

I had to admit, I was looking forward to this. It

was the ultimate 'fuck you' to Solomon Danforth for trying to kill us.

He'd surprised Boner and me, and had his minions bind us to a chair. Lucky I had something sharp on me, just in case. I'd freed myself and stabbed Danforth in the groin. I was aiming for slightly to the left, but it was effective in distracting him long enough for us two to get to him.

I won't lie. I was trying to work that into a play somehow, if I could do it without giving us all away. Who doesn't want to watch a play about a heroic playwright who saves his woman and her other boyfriends from certain death? Personally, I'd watch the hell out of that.

"Of course we do," Boner said with his typical cocky grin. "I always knew Cass, Hardbattle, and I would scrub up nice."

"Hard*wick*," I corrected. I couldn't tell if he was getting my name wrong on purpose or not, but I was going to keep reminding him until he got it through his thick skull.

Although, this one, as mistakes went, wasn't so bad. I made a note to use it when I wrote my play. Maybe Arnold Hardbattle? That sounded like a good protagonist name to me.

"Yeah, yeah." Boner flapped his hand in my direction. "We should get going. The party should be starting soon."

"Not without Harlow." Cass stepped over to take her hand, pulling her to him so they could walk together out the door.

"Definitely not without the guest of honor," Boner agreed. He opened the door and held it for the rest of us to file out. "Is Jules coming?" he asked as he closed it behind us.

"He said he'd meet us there," Cass said.

It was Jules we were talking about. He might decide not to show. The man was difficult and unpredictable, but Harlow liked him for some reason. They were constantly at each other's throats, but anyone could see the sparks flying between them. Sooner or later, she'd be calling him 'boyfriend' as well.

I wasn't sure how I felt about sharing her with another guy, but we'd made it work so far. I wasn't going to beat myself up about not staking my claim long before the rest of them came along. She wasn't ready for it then, and neither was I.

What changed? I wasn't sure. Possibly getting closer to the bottom of her list, like the light at the end of the proverbial tunnel. Psychology probably had something to say about that kind of optimism. Either way, we were here now, and I wasn't going to let her go.

Before we got onto the elevator to take us down to the street, I ordered us an Uber.

"It's only a couple of minutes away," I said. I caught a hint of regret in Boner and Cass' eyes.

Clearly they were thinking the same thing I was. We'd like to peel the dress off Harlow and make her scream a few times. If we were fashionably late to the opening, where was the harm?

We sighed in unison and stepped out of the elevator, arrayed around her like we were her bodyguards.

I could add that to my play. Playwright by day, bodyguard by night. Hero when required. Maybe I should think bigger. A screenplay instead of a play.

Before I could start thinking about who'd play me in the movie, the Uber pulled up in front of us.

"Your carriage awaits, my lady," Boner said grandly, opening the back door and gesturing for her to slide inside.

"It's not going to turn into a pumpkin at midnight, is it?" she said with a laugh.

"I hope not. Although, I'd make a cute mouse." Boner slid in beside her, leaving Cass to hurry around to the other door and me to slide into the front passenger seat.

"Of course you would," she said.

I twisted around and watched them kiss. His tongue slid over her lips and into her mouth.

If they kept doing that, Boner wasn't going to be the only boner around here. I'd have one in the front of my suit pants. Cass too, judging by the expression on his face, and the way the fabric rose, tenting in his lap.

The driver cleared his throat, confirmed the destination with me, and pulled away, narrowly missing running into another vehicle.

"Watch where you're going, asshole," he shouted out of the window, even though it was him who hadn't looked.

There was nothing like a hair-raising car ride to start the night.

Of course, if he got one of us killed, the rest of us would go after him. He didn't know that, and didn't seem intimidated by the glance I slid his way. Not surprising. There were more intimidating people in the city than me. On the outside, that was. He had no idea what I was like on the inside.

Which was why you should be careful who you pick up when driving an Uber.

Although I've seen that meme. The one that says one out of every four people is a serial killer. Since there were five of us in the car, the statistics weren't in his favor. I couldn't rule out the fact he was also one, but he wasn't going to be taking us to a side street and murdering us tonight. Or any other night, come to that.

The traffic crawled all the way to Angel's Redemption before the driver stopped in the middle of the street to let us out. I paid and followed the others past the line waiting outside, and into the restaurant.

"There's a line," Harlow said excitedly, looking over her shoulder with wide eyes.

"Of course there's a line," Boner said. "They'd be crazy not to stand out there for hours waiting to eat here."

"What he said," I agreed. Sometimes the man was wise. In this case, he was simply right.

The restaurant was popular before it was closed for renovations. People were waiting for it to reopen. Some would be regular customers. Others curious to see if it lived up to the hype, which it would, since it was Harlow's restaurant now.

I spotted a couple of food critics near the front of the line before I strode past them. I had no doubt they'd give her a good review. Before you ask, no I wasn't going to kill them if they didn't. Giving a bad review wasn't a good reason to murder someone. Or even maim them.

Usually.

One of Harlow's new staff met us inside the door

and led us over to a table with a card in the center that said, 'Reserved.'

I managed to maneuver myself so I was sitting beside Harlow with Cass on the other side. Boner huffed slightly before flopping down beside Cass.

I gave him the faintest of smirks. He couldn't sit next to her all the time. He busied himself pouring glasses of water for each of us from the jug in front of him, and passing them around. I nodded my thanks and took a sip. It was cold and refreshing and the glass was clean. Tick and tick.

As a stickler for cleanliness, I tended to notice these things. If a glass had stains on them, I always sent them back, especially lipstick stains. No offense to people who wear lipstick, but I don't want to wear it myself.

"I propose a toast." Boner raised his glass as if the water was fancy champagne. "To the most beautiful woman in the whole city. Harlow St. James."

I raised my own glass, and didn't offer any thoughts about his bias. If I did, I'd have to accept that I had my own bias. Fuck that. Harlow was the most beautiful woman in the city.

"To our woman," Cass said, looking at his glass like he hoped the water would turn into a milkshake.

Harlow must have been thinking the same thing I

was, because she laughed and reached over to put a hand on his bicep.

"We make milkshakes here," she assured him. "Wouldn't want you going without."

He grinned back at her. "You're the best."

The guy might pop, or implode, if he didn't get his hourly fix of the drink.

Personally, I couldn't see the appeal, but each to their own.

"I hope you don't mind, but the menu is set tonight," Harlow said. "I couldn't have opening night without serving my meatballs."

Cass, who'd just taken a sip of his water, almost choked on it. He started coughing, his hand thrown over his mouth.

"They only have beef and pork," she assured him.

He turned his face to give her a look, brow furrowed. "Promise?"

"I promise," she said with a nod. "Angel's Redemption is only going to serve the best ingredients."

Apparently that meant no bad guys on the menu. I was curious to see what bad guy tasted like, but not curious enough to try. Human flesh wasn't that good for you after all. It contained all sorts of bacteria and bad shit. Considering the source, they might have been tainted by evil too. Not that I believed in evil.

Not really. People usually had reasons for the things they did, even if they were completely horrible and fucked up.

I said reasons, not *good* reasons.

"I'm sorry to bother you, Harlow." The maitre d' stopped beside the table. "There's a man outside who says he knows you. We weren't sure if we should let him in."

Harlow's brow dipped briefly before she nodded her thanks. Only when her employee walked away did she turn and look at us. Her face slightly pale.

Had Hypnos or Zeus found us? Or Hans Getzoff come to arrest us?

She mouthed the word, "Fuck," before pushing herself to her feet and stepping toward the door.

# CHAPTER 5

## HARLOW

It was Archer who followed me to the door. I smelled his unique cologne. I didn't need to look back to know the others were close behind or keeping an eye on us, ready to act if necessary, but playing it cool for now. Nothing would say 'suspicious as fuck' like them standing around me like an angry honor guard.

I approached the door carefully. Certain no one would act against me with this many people around, but wishing I could back up my own certainty. If Hypnos and Zeus got desperate, they might do something drastic. Like show up at my restaurant and shoot me in the head.

Okay, not them personally, one of their hired guns.

I made my way past a group of customers who were heading into the restaurant.

I spotted a man in a suit as he turned to look at me. My heart stopped before I sagged in relief.

"Jules."

I should have known it was him. He glared at the security guard. A glare he quickly turned on me.

"Can you tell this gorilla I was invited?" he snapped.

I regarded him for a moment, during which I considered turning around and heading back into the restaurant. Let him stew in his own irritation for a while. Since I was in a good mood and didn't want to, I walked over to him, hips sashaying.

"I think it's safe to let you in," I said lightly.

He scoffed in response. His eyes still on me, he addressed the security guard, "I told you I knew her."

The guard looked at him like he'd happily throw him out on his ass anyway. "Just doing my job, bro." He turned back to the next person in line.

"You know saying things like that is no defense, right?" Archer asked from behind me. "Even if you say it to Jules"

"Fuck off," Jules snapped at him. He stuffed his hands into his pockets and made to step past me into the restaurant.

"It wouldn't hurt if you left your attitude at the door," I told him.

He glanced back and smirked. "My attitude comes with me wherever I go. Same as yours does."

Touché.

I hooked my arm in Archer's, and we walked back inside, taking our seats as Jules flopped down next to Cass.

"Ah, Titmus the elder," Boner said, giving him a grin. "It's about time you joined us. We were starting to think you stood us up."

"Thought about it," Jules admitted. "Cass wanted me here."

"We all want you here," Cass said, giving us all a look like we might contradict him, which, to be fair, we might. Jules was like that thorn in the side of your foot. The kind that itched at you, but for some reason you couldn't get it out.

"Yeah, we do," Boner agreed. "Jules is good for a laugh."

Jules placed his hand on the table in front of him, about to push himself to his feet.

I quickly reached out and grabbed his wrist. "We want you here," I insisted. "You know what Boner is like. If he's not stirring the pot, he's looking for a pot to stir."

Jules glanced at me. Then at Cass, who nodded. Finally he relaxed his pose and sat back.

"Fine, I'll stay. Maybe you should tell *him* to leave his attitude outside." He slid a cool look toward Boner.

"If I left my attitude outside, what would be left?" Boner spread his hands to either side. "I'm all attitude and personality, in case you hadn't noticed."

Jules muttered, "You're all something."

Boner grinned. "I love you too, bro. Look at us, all getting along like one big happy family. Go us."

"We are doing well," Archer agreed. "Considering most people with our…chosen hobby tend to be loners. We've broken that mold." Although he too glanced at Jules meaningfully.

Jules was doing a good impression of a loner who happened to be stuck in our company for the night.

"I'm glad you came," I told him. "It wouldn't be the same without all of us here." Nothing bonded people like almost being murdered. Not to mention finding employee spread around a restaurant floor. And walls. And tables.

"They're making Harlow's famous meatballs tonight," Cass supplied.

"Smells good already," Jules admitted.

He was right, it did. The aromas wafting from the kitchen made my stomach gurgle with appreciation.

Tonight's dinner would be a combination of old dishes and new, a hint of the former owner (not literally) and a whole lot of...me.

Also not literally.

As people shuffled in and made their way to their tables, a flutter of nerves passed through me. What if they didn't like the new menu? What if they ate here tonight and never came back?

"Everything is going to be perfect," Cass said.

Apparently I was wearing my thoughts on my face clear as day. I was usually better at masking my emotions. These four men must have found a way past those walls. At least they'd put ladders up so they could peek over the top.

"I know it will," I said, choking back unexpected emotion. "We've all worked hard to get here. I guess I'm a bit overwhelmed, that's all."

Was that a tear I wiped from underneath my eye? I wasn't usually a crier. I also didn't usually reopen a restaurant previously owned by my enemy, so I guessed it was a night for firsts.

"I bet Solomon Danforth is rolling over in his grave," Boner grinned.

If he had a grave. As far as I knew, he'd been cremated and his ashes scattered somewhere significant to his family. Just as well. I wouldn't put it past these guys, Boner in particular, to take a piss on his grave if they knew where it was.

Killing someone was one thing. Desecrating their grave was another. A girl had to draw the line somewhere. Apparently that was where I drew mine.

"He's not here, is he?" Jules looked around suspiciously, as if he might find a vase of ashes sitting on a shelf somewhere. Or a finger bone pointing in the direction of the toilets. Actually, that wasn't a bad idea. Not a real one though. That might make people a little suspicious.

"Only in spirit," I assured him.

Assuming spirits could stick their heads up from hell and have a look around at the pieces of their old lives. If that was the case, I mentally stuck up both my middle fingers at him.

*Look who won*, I thought.

He was dead and I was sitting at a very nice table in a very nice restaurant that used to have his name on the door.

"Success is the best revenge," Archer said.

"It really is," I agreed.

It was a shame Erin wasn't here to see it. To some extent, it was a shame Gina wasn't here to see it either, because fuck her for betraying me. Hopefully she had a nice little vantage point from hell as well.

Maybe she was sitting on Solomon's shoulders, telling him what she could see.

For some, those might be morbid thoughts, but for me, it was triumph. For now.

We still had to deal with—

"Hans Getzoff," Cass said suddenly.

"Lucky him. I mean where?" Boner asked, swiveling around in his seat.

"He just came through the door." Cass nodded.

I tried not to turn around and stare, but I ventured a glance back.

Getzoff stood with a woman around my age, both dressed to the nines like they were looking forward to a nice night out.

Hopefully that was all this was.

I tore my eyes away from him as he and his partner approached the table.

"Chef St. James," he said in a cheerful tone. "I've heard good things about your establishments. I thought I'd come check it out for myself."

I looked up at him and smiled, pretending I hadn't seen him until now, hoping I appeared genuine.

"Hello there, Mr…" I cocked my head slightly, waiting for him to give me his name.

"*Detective* Getzoff," he said smoothly. Just as

smooth as the night we met. "Hans Getzoff. This is my sister, Felicia."

I gave her a smile too.

"It's nice to meet you both. I hope you have a wonderful evening. If you have any problems, please let my maitre d' know. She'll pass it on to me."

I hope he got the message. He was more or less welcome here, but I didn't want him lurking around our table all night, disturbing me or the other customers in the restaurant.

"I'm sure I won't have anything to complain about," he said, his gaze lingering for a moment on my cleavage. "Have a nice evening." His arm around his sister's waist, he turned and walked in the direction of his own table.

"He gives me the creeps," Jules said.

"Me too," I said with a sigh.

Was it a coincidence he kept turning up in places where I also was? New York City was relatively small, especially if you moved in the same circles, but the way he looked at me gave me all sorts of creeps. Like he knew things I didn't want him to know. Or like he was trying to crawl underneath my skin and see how I ticked.

No thank you. I preferred to be the one looking under skin. I was firmly attached to mine.

"We could always...." Archer started, leaving the

words unsaid because we all knew what he was going to say.

"He hasn't done anything to us," I reminded him. "If he does, we can worry about it."

"Are you sure?" Boner was gazing thoughtfully in Getzoff's direction. "I don't know about you, but he gives me the heebie-jeebies. I'm always a big fan of being proactive and getting someone before they get you." He seemed ready to stand up, pick up a knife, and stab it right through Getzoff's carotid, not particularly caring he had an audience to witness the act.

I knew he wouldn't do something in public. We hadn't lasted this long without learning discretion. Me, Boner, and Archer in particular, since Cass and Jules were relatively new to this.

"He's a diner here to have dinner," I said firmly. "Nothing more."

"'We should keep an eye on him," Cass said, looking as worried as Boner.

"I one hundred percent agree with that," Jules said, leaning his elbows on the table.

"Of course," I said. "We'll keep an eye on him, but we won't do anything unless he gives us a good reason."

I looked around at them, hoping they were listening. *Really* listening.

They all had their moments of unpredictability. I

didn't need them going off the rails and after a police detective. Not if we ended up under the microscope.

If they found out what we were up to, we were screwed. And if they didn't, having them breathe down our necks would make it that much more difficult to go after Hypnos and Zeus.

No, we had to keep a low profile. Keep our noses clean, and stay out of the way of Getzoff.

The conversation ended with the rattle of plates and the servers placing our first course in front of us.

The discussion wasn't over, but for now we could enjoy our meal. Or try to anyway.

It was difficult when I felt as though Getzoff's eyes were on me the entire time.

# CHAPTER 6

## HARLOW

"That was exhilarating," I said as the last of the staff left and I closed the door behind them.

"We can call that a rousing success," Boner declared. "Everyone had a great time and the food was amazing."

"So good," Cass agreed, sucking down the last of his milkshake.

"The sauce could have used a bit more basil," Jules remarked.

"I disagree." Archer propped his elbows on the table and rested his face on his hands. "It was perfectly balanced and flavorsome."

"Did you swallow an encyclopedia, or fuck one?" Jules asked.

"While eating a small amount of paper isn't bad

for you," Archer said, "an entire encyclopedia would give me a stomachache. As for the logistics of fucking one…"

Jules waved a hand in front of his face. "You know what? Forget it. I should have known you'd take it literally."

The side of Archer's mouth twitched, his version of a grin. Amused that he'd scored points off Jules.

"How much paper do you have to eat to make yourself sick?" Cass asked. "Asking for a friend."

"I'd say you have some fucked up friends, but that's obvious," Jules told him.

"You're here with us too," I reminded him.

Boner pointed a finger right at his nose. "Don't tell me you're not enjoying yourself because we all know you'd be lying. You're having as good a time tonight as the rest of us. You just don't show it the way some of us do."

Jules grunted in response. "It was okay. I've had worse nights."

"And worse company." Boner gave him a 'come on' gesture to admit we weren't that bad.

"That too, I guess." Jules said as he scrubbed a hand over his face. "Should one of us be following Getzoff?

"Are you volunteering?" I asked gently.

The detective and his sister were one of the last to

leave. He gave me a long look before he followed her out the door. The hairs on the back of my neck hadn't settled down again yet.

"We should stay away from him until I do a background search on him," Cass said before Jules could respond.

"It's a good idea to know your enemy before you go after them," Boner agreed.

"We don't know that he's our enemy," I pointed out. "He could just be a creep." He wouldn't be the first or the last.

"He's my enemy," Boner said. "Anyone who looks at you the way he does, and isn't sitting at this table, is on my shit list."

"Okay, but there's a difference between being jealous and going after someone because they're a bad person," I said.

"Are you saying I'm not on your shit list?" Jules said to Boner.

"I did say that, didn't I?" Boner tilted his head to the side and frowned thoughtfully. "What's the next step up from shit list? Acquaintance list?" His eyes shone. Clearly Jules was higher than that, but he too couldn't resist scoring points off him.

"Can you all just be friends?" Cass said softly. "It wouldn't kill you."

"It might," Boner said cheerfully.

"Have you forgotten I saved your ass when Solomon Danforth had you tied to a fucking chair?" Jules snapped. "Next time, I'll leave you there."

"And if you're ever—" Boner started.

"Enough," I insisted. "No one is leaving anyone tied to a chair without their consent."

"So…with their consent is okay?" Boner asked.

Of course that was what he took away from it.

"Whatever you want to do, with consent, is up to you," I said. "Are you trying to tell me you have a chair kink, Edward Bonegard?" I arched my eyebrows at him. "Or bondage?"

Boner sighed. "Honestly, before that night I would have said I'm open to anything and everything. Now, the idea of being tied up to a chair isn't all that appealing, believe it or not." He glanced down toward the top of the table, his eyes glazed. That night must have been more traumatic than he let on. He kept it hidden behind his usual cheerful demeanor, pretending he was okay when he wasn't.

I put a hand over his and squeezed. "I believe it," I said gently. "It must have been scary."

"Part scary, part boring as fuck," Boner agreed. "If it wasn't for Archer, I might still be attached to that chair, waiting for someone to find us all. Our corpses half-rotten. Bugs eating us. Our…"

"All right. We get the picture." I said quickly, putting my hand up in front of my face.

That was a visual image I didn't need in my brain. I knew one day we'd all die, but I didn't want to think about lying dead in an apartment for six months, no one knowing we were there.

Although, was that possible?

My staff would notice if I didn't turn up to work. So would Boner's. Someone would come looking for us. Would they have found us in Archer's place? The whole idea of staying there was so no one knew where we were. No one but people I thought I could trust.

"If you don't have me cremated when I die, I'm going to haunt you," Jules said to Cass.

"Same, bro, same," Cass said back. His skin looked slightly green. Evidently thinking of himself decomposing like that was sickening for him, too.

"So, you had a suggestion for a playdate after the opening?" I said, directing the question to Boner, hoping to put the grisly thoughts behind us.

"I did," Boner agreed, pouncing on the change of topic with glee. As glad as the rest of us to move on to someone else's grisly death instead of ours.

Boner pulled out his phone and opened the screen. "Lionel Gammage was a teacher…"

"Someone beat us to it," I said, although the words were redundant.

Lionel Gammage lay on the floor in the middle of his apartment, eyes open and staring.

"Not by much." Archer crouched beside him to take a closer look at the blood pooled around Gammage's open throat. He placed a hand on his wrist. "He's barely started to cool."

"So what you're saying is we snuck up a fire escape and into this guy's apartment and barely missed whoever murdered him?" Jules asked, lingering near the window.

"They might still be here," I pointed out. A fact which immediately put everyone on edge.

"I'll take a look around." Boner slid out his knife and made his way through the apartment. Looking behind doors. Inside closets. Even under the bed.

"There's no one here. No one *else* here," he amended, as if we were about to be smartasses and correct him the same way he would have done if it was one of us speaking.

He put his knife away and grimaced down at the dead man. "I have to admit, this is disappointing. This isn't the date I promised my woman."

I put an arm over his shoulders. "It's okay, it's the

thought that counts. At least someone took care of him."

"Yeah, but who?" Cass picked up Gammage's phone and started to look through it.

"We might have some competition," Boner suggested. He actually seemed to like the idea.

"We're not starting a game between us and another killer," I told him.

"*We* aren't, but what about them?" The Englishman gestured toward Gammage. "They're the ones who started it."

I gave him a stern look. "This isn't the playground. We can't run off to teacher and say, 'They started it.'" I raised my voice to a child like pitch.

"Who do we run off to, then?" Boner asked, grinning.

"I vote we get the hell out of here and call this one in to the cops," I said.

"Too late." Archer pushed himself to his feet. It wasn't until he was standing that I realized what he was referring to. The sound of sirens was common in the city, but these seemed to be heading straight toward us.

I could put it down to paranoia, but the sound made me want to bolt.

"One 'getting the hell out of here' coming up," Boner said.

Jules was the first to climb back out of the window and start down the fire escape. The other three herded me toward it, all but pushing me out before they followed me. We barely made it down to the ground before a couple of police cars rounded the corner and stopped in front of the building.

Keeping to the shadows as much as possible, we moved away, only stopping when we got a safe distance. I glanced back over my shoulder as an all too familiar figure stepped out of one of the cars.

"Isn't that interesting?" Boner said slowly. "What are the statistical possibilities of Detective Getzoff being here right now? He glanced over at Archer.

"Small," Archer said simply.

"How the hell did they know?" Jules whispered. He glared at Boner. "You were the one who brought us here."

"I did. But I'm not crazy enough to put myself in harm's way," Boner said. "And I wouldn't risk Harlow. Or the rest of you."

He glanced at Cass for a moment and gave him a quick smile. They hadn't discussed what was growing between them, but it was obvious to anyone who looked. They were adorable together. I was all for them exploring all the possibilities.

"Thanks for bringing me along for the ride,"

Getzoff was saying to one of the other cops. "That tip-off sounded suspicious as hell."

The uniformed cop gave him a glance and a shrug, irritated. Not caring about the detective's gratitude. He was here to do his job, and evidently he was about to get his toes stepped on. I'd be annoyed too. They disappeared into the building.

"Who tipped them off?" Jules asked.

Cass was tapping away at his own phone. "I can't find any evidence of cameras. It's possible Gammage screamed."

He didn't look like he believed that. Neither did I, to be honest.

Someone could have been watching. I saw no sign of anyone peering between their curtains or standing out on the street pointing fingers. If there were, they would have drawn a crowd by now. Either on the street or with people watching out their windows. Who could resist a spectacle like that?

"It's possible the real perpetrator called in the tip," Boner said.

"Right," Archer agreed. "That's possible for two reasons. One, he wanted the attention from the police. That's common with serial killers; they like to be noticed."

"Called out," Boner muttered.

"The other possibility is they're messing with us,"

I concluded. I rubbed a hand over my forehead, then massaged my temples.

"Only if they knew we'd be here." Jules looked accusingly at Boner again.

"I didn't tell them," Boner insisted. "Gammage was facing a raft of charges. It's possible someone intercepted the same information I did. I mean, we can't be the only ones trying to do the right thing around here, right?"

None of us had the answer to that question.

"How many coincidences can a person have before it's not a coincidence anymore?" I asked. "Whatever we do, Getzoff turns up. Or something happens that brings him into our proximity. What are we missing?"

Had someone betrayed us again? Was it one of the men standing close to me? One of my new staff? I couldn't rule out the possibility Hypnos or Zeus found us and were playing cat and mouse with us, laughing their asses off as we stumbled around trying to figure out which way was up.

"I'm missing having private time with my woman," Boner said adjusting his blonde man bun. "Let's get out of here before they start searching the neighborhood for a killer."

Jules snorted at the irony, but was quick enough to follow us away from the crime scene.

# CHAPTER 7

HARLOW

We were barely inside the door of Archer's apartment before Boner dragged his lips over mine. He bracketed my hips with his hands and pulled me to him, our chests bumping together. His tongue slid between my lips, mine tangled with his, tasting the tang of tomatoes and garlic with a hint of beer.

Cass stepped around beside me and gripped the zipper of my dress, dragging it down slowly. The straps slid down my arms, stopping when they reached Boner's wrists.

"You have the most incredible nipples," Boner remarked, leaning back to get a good look.

"Yours aren't so bad yourself," I told him, starting to undo the buttons on his shirt but leaving his tie in place. When I had enough undone, I slipped my hands inside, over his taut abs. Up his chest to tease his nipples.

Jules stepped past us, glancing down at my chest. Then back to my face. "I should…" He started inching away.

"You can stay if you want," I told him. I wanted him here, but if he was uncomfortable with us, I'd let him go. The choice had to be his.

His tongue slid over his lower lip.

"Maybe I'll stick around for a while."

I gave him a smile as Boner lifted his hands from my hips and let my dress fall to the floor.

"Commando," he remarked, taking in my bare pussy.

"In that dress? Of course." I nodded down towards the puddle on the floor.

"If I knew that, I would have come in my pants while we were having dinner," Cass said, before instantly regretting his words. Red crept up his neck and across his face.

Boner leaned over to pat his shoulder. "Same, bro. Same."

"Figures you're a two-pump chump," Jules said, directing the remark to Boner. Either ignoring or oblivious to the fact he basically insulted his brother as well.

"You say that like it's a bad thing," Boner said,

clearly not offended. "Have you seen this woman? Who wouldn't be crazy aroused by her? I get hard looking at her little finger." He grabbed my hand and held it up to show everyone. "I mean, look at that finger." He gestured toward it with his hand.

"It's just a finger," I said with a laugh.

Boner brought it to his lips and kissed it. "It's a beautiful finger, like the rest of you." He paused for a moment before saying, "The rest of you is beautiful, you're not a finger."

Without warning, he ducked down, scooped me up in his arms, and carried me over to the couch.

I only managed a squeak of protest and then he was putting me down and kneeling between my legs. There was no protest left in me when he lowered his face to my pussy and started to devour me like I was second dessert.

Cass sat down on one side of me and, to my surprise, Jules sat down on the other. Both with hungry gazes. When Cass lowered his mouth to trace circles around my nipples, Jules looked like he wanted to do the same.

"It's okay," I told him. "I want you to touch me."

He hesitated for a moment longer, before reaching out and running the pad of his thumb over my other nipple, making it hard enough to slice through his skin.

I quivered. Both brothers touching me in such a sensitive place sent heat straight down to my core. It pooled there, rising with every stroke of Boner's tongue.

"I'm starting to think I'm in the wrong job," Archer said, his voice low and husky. "I should move into writing and directing adult entertainment."

He certainly seemed to be enjoying what he was watching. His suit pants were open, pushed down far enough for him to wrap his fingers around his cock. He stroked it gently and slowly. His jaw clenched like he was trying to hold himself back, while his body desperately sought release.

Slowly, Boner lifted his mouth off me and turned to look at Archer. "Are you saying I should have been a porn star?" He grinned and quickly turned back to lavish more attention on my clit.

"No way," Cass said, lifting his mouth off me and replacing it with his fingers. "I'm not sharing her with the rest of the world."

"There's more than enough porn on the internet as there is," Archer said.

"How much is there?" Jules asked, giving him a sideways glance as if daring him to answer the question.

"Enough," was Archer's response. Either he didn't

have an approximate number or that wasn't a priority right now. Possibly both.

Apparently Jules was satisfied with that answer because he looked away, returning his attention to my nipple. That little nub of skin and nerves seemed to be the most fascinating thing he'd ever seen. His gaze was intent there.

Any other time I might have asked him if he'd never seen a nipple before, but I didn't want to spar with him right now. There were other things I wanted to do. Not to mention the blood was rushing out of my brain, through my body and into my core.

Who needed to think when you could feel?

I leaned back and half-closed my eyes. Ground myself against Boner's stubble, pushing me hard and fast towards orgasm.

I came with a cry, rolling my hips harder as I was swallowed whole by a wave of bliss. Compounded by Cass's mouth on my nipple and Jules pinching the other between his thumb and forefinger. It hurt, but in the best way.

All four of them hesitated, glancing at each other before Cass sat up straight and took charge.

He regarded his brother for a moment before saying, "Archer, come here and fuck her."

Archer quickly shed the rest of his clothes and took Boner's place in front of me. He gripped my waist and pulled me onto his cock, sliding into me in one smooth stroke.

"Boner," Cass said, his eyes dark. He shed his own clothes and gestured for the Englishman to kneel in front of him while he perched beside me.

"Yes, Cass?" Boner asked, his eyes shining.

Cass smirked, knowing Boner understood what he was asking. "Suck my dick."

"With pleasure," Boner placed his hands on Cass' thighs and all but swallowed his cock.

Jules muttered something about Cass being a bossy prick, but then he was undoing the front of his own pants and wrapping his fingers around his cock.

"Don't work yourself too much," his younger brother told him. "You're going to fuck Harlow next."

Jules' whole body jerked. I thought he was going to come then and there. He opened his mouth like he might argue with Cass, but shrank back again.

He wanted to fuck me as much as I wanted to fuck him.

I raised my legs and placed my feet to either side of me on the couch, opening me wider so Archer could drive in deeper.

"Fuck, Harlow," he said breathlessly. His thrusts became harder and faster—frantic, like this might be the last chance we'd ever have for him to be inside me.

The deliberate, contained man was gone for now, replaced by urgency. Almost like he was acutely aware of our mortality. Seeing Gammage lying there dead tonight might have reminded him, but he wasn't unaware in the first place.

I didn't know when he started killing, but it was long enough ago that he knew each day could be his last.

I moaned and whispered his name. I wanted all of him as far inside me as he could get; deeper, harder, more.

"Just like that," I whispered as he hit all the way inside my pussy, smashing his way into me over and over.

"Come inside her," Cass ordered, his voice as breathless as mine. His eyes were half closed, watching me, while Boner sucked and licked his cock and stroked his balls. His whole body was tense like he was just about to shatter.

"Come inside him," I managed to say right before another orgasm hit me. This one tearing through me like wildfire, igniting me until I was ready to burn down to ashes.

I tilted my head back and screamed at the ceiling, my cries mingling with Archer's, then Cass' as they both came apart.

My head finally cleared as Boner slid his mouth off Cass' cock with a pop.

"That was hot," Boner said.

"Yeah, it was," Jules said agreed, his voice strained.

Then he was trading places with Archer. Pulling me off the couch and turning me around so I lay across the couch cushions, my ass to him.

He gripped my hips and drove himself all the way to the hilt, hard enough to hurt us both.

I cried out in pain and surprise, mixed with a healthy hint of pleasure.

"You like it rough?" He leaned forward to whisper in my ear. When I hummed my agreement, he slapped his hand down on my ass so hard it stung.

I cried out again. He slapped me once, twice, harder each time. Hard enough that tears sprang to my eyes, but I didn't pull away.

He grabbed my wrists and pulled them behind my back, holding them with one hand while he pounded into me.

"Tell me you hate this," he whispered. "Tell me you hate me."

I turned my face as Cass knelt down in front of Boner and took the Englishman's cock between his lips.

"I hate you," I told Jules. "I hate this."

"Do you want me to stop?" His voice was gravelly with lust.

"No," I said. Apparently that was the wrong answer. He slapped my ass again. Harder still.

"Yes," I said pleadingly. "I want you to stop."

I didn't want him to stop, not for a moment. If this was his game, I was here to play it.

"Beg me," he insisted.

I blinked away real tears and looked back at him. "Please. Please stop."

The grin he gave me was brutal, as brutal as the pounding he was giving my pussy.

He leaned forward and whispered, "I'm not going to fucking stop. You deserve this. You deserve everything I give you. You're a fucking whore. You should be on your fucking knees all day. Like the bitch whore you are."

I moaned again. His dirty talk was driving me towards a third orgasm.

"Please," I said again, this time begging him to keep going. To fuck me hard so I could come again.

Still holding my wrist with one hand, he grabbed a fistful of hair in the other, dragging my head back and driving harder into me.

"The first time I saw you, I knew you were a slut," he said harshly. "Is there anyone you wouldn't spread your legs for?"

"Yes," I cried out. "I wouldn't spread them for you."

He barked a vicious laugh and pounded into me until I came for a third time, harder and higher than the last two. Screaming out his name until my throat was raw.

He slammed into me a couple more times before, letting out a roar of his own and coming inside me. The salt of his cum stung my skin, reminding me I was alive.

When he finally released my hair, I flopped down, pressing my cheek against the couch cushion and trying to clear my mind.

While I panted, Boner came, Cass stroking his cock with his lips and tongue.

Jules sagged down over me and gathered me up in his arms like an apology. "Are you okay?" he said in my ear, so only I could hear.

"Better than okay," I assured him. "It was perfect."

"Does Archer have a bath that doesn't have acid?" he asked, although he knew the answer. He'd been living here for the last six months, along with the rest of us. After the attack, we hadn't talked about it; we just hadn't left.

I laughed softly. "As a matter of fact…"

Just as well. I could do with one right now.

# CHAPTER 8
## BONER

I know this is Archer's book, but I've never had my cock sucked by another man. For the record, I liked it. He and Harlow could suck me anytime.

Also, don't tell Jules, but the way he banged her was hot as fuck.

————

Archer

If you're familiar with Clifton Strengths, it won't surprise you to know I'm number one Intellection. That means I think a lot. It's hard to turn my brain off. That might also be my autism speaking. When I sit down to work, I can stay still for hours.

Like tonight. After everyone went to bed, I sat down at my desk and started writing. The ideas flowed out of me like fresh blood. Although, from the first word, they headed in a totally different direction from what I intended. I rolled with it.

Believe me, I could have written a detailed description of Harlow's body and the way she looked and sounded when she fucked. I watched her closely, taking in every single detail, committing them to memory.

Instead, I focused on the screen in front of me. Dialogue and description. The nuances in her voice when she spoke. The flash of her smile. References to her freckles. So many references to those.

"What are you working on?" I didn't know Harlow got up until she placed a cup of coffee beside me. The steam rose off the surface, the aroma soothing and stimulating at the same time.

"The next big thing." I gave her a nod of thanks. "I might win an Oscar for this one."

"I don't know how I feel about that." She leaned against the edge of the desk. "On one hand, I'd love that for you. On the other, if this is about me…"

"You don't want the scrutiny." It wasn't a question.

I knew she didn't. She was taking enough of a risk increasing her profile with two restaurants.

This could thrust her into the limelight faster than my dick into her wet, ready pussy. With the limelight came fans, people watching and cataloguing her every move, taking candid photos, stalking her social media.

Stalking *her*.

"If you don't want me to finish it, I won't," I said. I tapped my fingers on the desktop as I thought.

"I'll make changes so no one will know it's you. My protagonist could be a ballet dancer or work in a pet shelter."

I'd have to give her fewer freckles. That made me so uncomfortable I shifted in my seat. I had a picture in my mind of what she looked like. Deviating from that took adjustment.

"That's probably a good idea," she agreed, visibly grateful I made the offer.

"Is it?" I twisted around and looked up at her. "When we find Hypnos and Zeus, will we need to keep killing?" That wasn't the simple question it seemed to be on the surface. Hunting and killing was all but ingrained on us at this point. Other people took holidays. We took lives.

She pursed her lips. "I don't know. Part of me

would like to put all of that behind me, focus on my restaurants and living my life."

"But part of you remembers they're two monsters out of many," I said for her.

She drew in a long breath through her nose and exhaled softly. "Exactly. I wish I could snap my fingers and they'd all, I don't know, shrivel up and die."

I managed a slight laugh in the back of my throat. "That would surprise a lot of people. When a bunch of men around them, and women too, disappeared into dust."

"That's the thing, isn't it?" she said slowly. "They *would* be surprised. Not all of them, but some. Plenty. People like Hypnos and Zeus are good at hiding in plain sight."

"Yes, they are," I agreed. "But we're better." We had to be. We were outnumbered by monsters.

"I hope we are," she said. "But if someone is trying to mess with us, maybe we're not as good as we think." Her eyes were laced with worry.

"Are you wishing you stuck to working alone?" I asked.

Having three others along for the ride was new for me as well. I wasn't sure I'd adjusted quite yet. Jules said he wasn't a people person, but neither was

I. I was good at masking and pretending I was almost as social as those around me.

Maybe I should be more like him and be grumpy. Keep people at arm's length with my personality. I couldn't though, it wasn't who I was.

Besides, I liked having Harlow around. As long as I got some time to myself when I needed it, I'd be okay.

"No," she said slowly. "It is riskier, but I like that you all have my back. Not that I didn't enjoy it when it was just you backing me up."

Slowly and slightly, I raised an eyebrow at her, then the other. "Who was backing who up?"

She smiled. She baited me and I'd walked right into it.

"We were backing each other up," she said quickly, as if somehow she might have offended me.

I wasn't that easy to offend.

"Yes, we were." I reached for her hand, curling my fingers around hers.

Her skin was smooth and smelled good. Her scent today like frangipani and lilac. Soft and tropical. Appropriate for her. Soft and warm when she wanted to be. Hot and steamy when she needed.

Nothing about this woman was simple, straightforward or uncomplicated. She was fascinating and complex, wrapped in a skin of beauty and perfection.

Yes, I know that sounds flowery, but I *am* a playwright and screenwriter after all. Flowery prose is my bread and butter.

Harlow was the sweet strawberry jelly on top, maybe with a hint of peanut butter. The smooth kind, not the crunchy. I hated the texture of crunchy peanut butter. It was almost as bad as overripe banana and soufflé. Yuck.

"I love you," I whispered so quietly I barely heard my own words. "I've loved you since the day we met." Before she could be facetious and correct me, I said, "The night we met," and smirked.

She smiled, letting me know I was right about what she was going to say.

"I love you too," she whispered back. "That was a hell of a night, wasn't it?"

"Oscar Hetherington," I said thinking back. "The third man on your list."

"Yes, he was." Her eyes were glazed, thinking back too.

"After the first two, I thought I knew what I was doing. He proved me wrong. He knew we were coming."

"He knew *you* were coming," I corrected, not from conceit, but because it was a fact. I liked facts. Precision.

"Right." She nodded slowly. "He knew I was coming. He was ready."

"And then I showed up and made things more difficult," I said.

"You showed up and made things *easier*." Now she was the one correcting me. "If you hadn't come in when you did, he would have shot me and we wouldn't be having this conversation."

"That depends what happens after we die," I said, "If he'd shot you, I would have been next. We might be in the afterlife, talking about how bad our timing was."

She laughed at that. "I suppose that's possible."

"Do you ever think about it?" I asked. "What comes next?"

She took another long, slow breath. "I think about it, but I don't have any conclusions. As far as I know, there's only one way to find out what comes next, and I'm not ready for that yet. When I am, I'll report back and let you know."

"You will not die before I do." I managed to put almost as much growl in my voice as one of her other boyfriends. "If you die, then I better be dead already."

She turned her hand around and laced our fingers together.

"I was going to say the same to you. I couldn't imagine my life without all of you in it."

"Including Jules," I said, teasing lightly.

"Including him," she agreed.

Lucky for all concerned, she didn't add, 'especially him.' I didn't mind the guy, but I didn't want to be an afterthought.

"You liked him being rough with you," I said.

Her lips turned up in a soft smile.

"I did. It felt good. And I know he enjoyed himself."

"Do me a favor," I said, locking my eyes on her. "Don't forget to put yourself first once in a while." When she started to argue, I cut her off with a glance.

"You're always thinking about other people. The innocent people you want to save. People you want vengeance for, like your sister. Your customers. Us. Sometimes Harlow St. James deserves to put Harlow St. James front and center."

"I'll think about it," she promised. "As long as you do the same."

"I do," I assured her. "I need time to myself to get my work done, for one thing."

For my sanity, for another. What does the meme say? The collective noun for a group of humans is a 'fuck nope.'

Four other people in my life was the right amount. Any more and I was going to have to insist we buy a large house in the Hamptons where I could have my own wing. That didn't sound so bad when I thought about it. I might look into that later.

"I've probably disturbed you enough," she said, realizing we'd been talking for a while. "I should leave you alone."

"It's okay," I said quickly. "I don't mind being sidetracked by you for a while."

I glanced at the screen to check the time. Blinked when I saw how much of it was gone. It was about two in the morning when I sat down here to start working. It was now almost seven. Definitely time for a break.

"Are you going to get some sleep?" she asked, giving me a worried look.

I rubbed the heel of my hand over my forehead. "After breakfast, I will," I assured her.

While the others were at work, I'd lie down and catch up with a nap. Fortunately, both my job and my hobby allowed me to operate at night and sleep during the day because I was *not* a daylight person. My mother used to joke that I was a vampire, but I preferred the dark and quiet of night. The solitude. The time to think without comings and goings from the people in the apartments around me. Not that they didn't come and go at all hours, but less so at night.

Sometimes I'd sit on the rooftop terrace and look

out across the city. Pretend I had the whole space to myself. Up high and alone was a good place to refill the creative well in my mind. To think about nothing in particular and let the ideas come to me. Sometimes work with existing ideas until I was happy with them.

Now, I wanted to sit and look at Harlow. In the past, the city was my muse; now she was. The ideas she'd inspired since I met her were like nothing I'd had before. Likely none I'd have again. As long as I lived, I wanted to be around her, to let my imagination go wild with thoughts of her.

"Your coffee is getting cold," she reminded me.

Reluctantly, I opened my hand to let her pull hers back. The moment her skin wasn't touching mine, I felt empty.

Curling my hand around the cup of coffee did almost nothing to fill the vacuum. Coffee was good but there were things it couldn't do. Replace her was one of them. Especially not when, as she said, my coffee was almost cold.

"I'll get you another one," she said.

I shook my head. "No, I'll get you one."

"I tell you what, whoever gets to the kitchen first gets to make the coffee."

She grinned and started off on a run, her bare feet thudding on the hardwood floor.

# CHAPTER 9

## HARLOW

"Don't look now," Cass said, taking the dirty plates off the servery countertop and carrying them over to the sink to rinse them.

"What am I not looking at?" I turned the handle on the pasta maker while keeping half an eye on two pots of sauce.

"Hans Getzoff just walked through the door." Cass held a fork in his hand, a little too long and a little too much like he might stab Getzoff through the eye with it.

"Nothing we can't handle," I said lightly. "Just act normal."

He placed the fork into the dishwasher and washed his hands more vigorously than usual.

I snorted. "As normal as we can." That wasn't too much to ask, right? We were relatively normal on the outside. It wasn't until you scratched the surface that you found what was going on underneath. If you scratched hard enough.

Granted, I didn't let other people close enough to do it, most of the time.

"Try to act normal. Got it," he said with a nod of his head. "Um, what is that again?"

The smile on his face was half amusement, half panic. Eyes flicking back toward the seating area.

"When I figure it out, I'll let you know," I quipped. "I think it means do your job and don't panic."

"Work and don't panic," he said slowly. "Okay, I can do those." He seemed relatively certain of that at least.

"You should probably stay in the kitchen too," I added. "The less he sees of us, the better."

"Unless—" Cass started to say.

"Chef St. James." Getzoff appeared at the kitchen door.

"Detective Getzoff," I said with more enthusiasm than I felt. "How nice to see you again."

I was lying through my teeth, but that was a small crime compared to other things I'd done, so I figured the universe might let it slide.

"What brings you here?" I asked.

My heart thumped too hard in my chest. Almost to the point of pain. Not the good kind either, worse luck. Not like when Jules fucked me, so perfectly hard.

Was Getzoff was about to accuse me of something? Maybe the death of Lionel Gammage? Maybe feeding victims to my customers. Maybe…

I couldn't think of anything else. My mind was racing too fast.

"I enjoyed your food so much the other night, I thought I'd pop in and try the food here," he said lightly.

"That's very flattering," I said sincerely.

I didn't have to bullshit my way through this one. I was proud of my cooking. I'd worked hard to develop my skills. This was a compliment I could comfortably accept, even from someone who gave me the creeps.

"I'm sure Shelly will be more than happy to show you to a table and take your order," I said, which was a not-so-subtle hint for him to step away and leave me to my work, both in the restaurant and after hours.

"You're not going to show me around yourself?" he asked, his tone slick, like he'd put too much butter on his personality bread.

I must be hanging around Boner too much. That

was the kind of observation he'd make. Along with something like, 'It's never a good idea to overdo the lubrication. Or underdo it.'

I almost heard his voice in my head, saying that and laughing. If he was here right now, he'd defuse the situation so much better than I could.

I forced a smile. "There's not much to see. This is the kitchen. That's the seating area." I gestured from one to the other.

"So I see." Getzoff took another step further inside, scanning the kitchen with his intense blue eyes, as if he could see through the cabinetry, or past the fridge door to the contents. As if somehow the dishwasher would reveal something incriminating about me.

"We passed our health inspection the other day," I said, pretending to assume he was checking for cleanliness before he sat down to eat.

I won't lie, I have had customers insist on inspecting the kitchen before they committed to a meal.

"I'm sure you did," he said, his eyes stopping on Cass for a moment before returning to me. "I'm sure you thoroughly clean your workspace."

He said it so carefully, deliberately, I was ready to choke on air.

Apparently so was Cass, since he had a sudden coughing fit. He threw his hand over his mouth and leaned away into the corridor that led to the back door of the restaurant.

"Our hygiene here is second to none," I said firmly. "You could eat off the floor."

I had a sudden vision of Getzoff, chained to one of the tables, doing just that. Begging to be released. Insisting he wouldn't arrest and lock us up.

I shoved the image away. The last thing I wanted was to detain a police officer, especially here. One person strolling by, one casual peer in the window, they'd see him.

No, that was a bad idea for so many reasons.

Getzoff glanced down at the floor. "That would be an interesting dining experience."

"Yes, it would," I agreed, keeping my tone as congenial as possible. "I don't think it'll catch on, though. People like the comfort of a good chair and a table."

"Yes, a good chair is definitely a must," he said, injecting meaning into it I couldn't quite figure out.

Was there any way he knew about Solomon Danforth tying Boner and Archer to chairs?

Not unless one of us told him. Solomon's minions weren't around to tell the tale.

No, Getzoff was guessing, but I didn't know why or how it was so specific.

*I'm being paranoid*, I told myself. *He's making small talk. I'm reading things into it that aren't there.*

Was it a police detective thing, to speak in a way that made people twitch? As if they'd confess some great crime after he put on the back foot?

*Good luck with that.* I wasn't going to be back-footed so easily.

"I can show you to a table if you like," I said. "Then I really should get back to work."

I'd stopped turning the handle. I started again now. Winced when the pasta came out the other end slightly wonky. I cursed myself. I'd have to put it through again. Yes, no one would know when it was buried under sauce, but *I'd* know. The imperfection would drive me up the wall.

"That's not necessary." Getzoff gave me a smile as though he was being generous in some way. Like leaving me to get back to my job was a big deal for him.

I managed to contain a bristle. Men who were full of their own importance also drove me up the wall. It didn't matter what someone looked like on the outside. If they were arrogant on the inside, they weren't my type.

Smooth as hell wasn't my type either, to be honest. I liked my men a little rough around the edges. Who didn't look at me like I climbed a ladder and stabbed the moon to death.

People, yes, not the moon.

Getzoff gave Cass another long look, then turned and walked over to the table beside the window. He pulled out the chair for himself and sat down before picking up the menu and scanning it.

"Have you ever poisoned anyone?" Cass asked in my ear, making me startle.

"What? No." I turned around quickly. "For one thing, that could be traced back to us. For another, he hasn't done anything wrong."

"Not yet," Cass said on an exhale. "You know he's going to, though. He has that look."

I wanted to ask what look, but instead I nodded.

"He really does." I pressed the back of my hand to his chest, over his heart and whispered "Someone like Granger Fairfield."

Cass glanced down at me, then back at the detective. "Yeah, exactly. He's got that 'I can do whatever the fuck I want, and no one can stop me' thing going on."

"That still doesn't mean he's up to something," I pointed out.

He hadn't accused us of anything. Didn't pull out a badge and insist on searching the place.

Of course, he'd need a search warrant for that. Honestly, I'd be happy for him to search the place to his heart's content. He wouldn't find anything here. I was much too careful for that.

Besides, it was months since anyone came through here and ended up on the menu.

"I ran a check on him." Cass picked up a washcloth to wipe the counter that didn't need wiping. "Nothing came up. He was top of his class. One of the youngest detectives in the city, yada yada. Clean as…"

"As this place," I suggested.

"Cleaner." His lips twisted in irritation.

I knew Cass hoped to find something. All of the guys wanted an excuse to go after Getzoff and get him off our backs. If we could do that without being caught.

"He knows something," Cass said, tossing the washcloth aside. "I don't know what it is, but he knows something."

"I get that impression too," I admitted.

As long as we played it cool, he wouldn't learn anything about us. If I kept looking panicked when he appeared, sooner or later he'd figure out something was up.

"Harlow." Shelly stepped over to the servery. "The customer at table four wants something that's not on the menu." She looked apologetic.

"Of course he does. What is he asking for?"

"He's requesting lasagna," she said. "I told him it's not available today, but he's insisting."

"I'll rustle some up," I assured her. "Let him know it'll take a little bit extra time."

She nodded, "Yes, Chef."

Cass looked over at me from where he stood in front of the sink.

"You know what Boner would say to that."

I snorted. "Yes, I do, but it's still not grounds to… *ground* someone." Difficult customers were a dime a dozen around here. I lost count of the amount of times I'd been asked for things that weren't on the menu. Fortunately, this was one I could rectify quickly enough.

I grabbed another ball of pasta dough out of the fridge and made lasagna sheets to throw together with the Bolognese sauce.

I'd left it off the menu for the last few weeks to give it a rest. I liked to keep things interesting and fresh. There was a chance I was overthinking it. Should I add it back on? People would order it.

Although I suspected he would have asked for something else instead.

While the lasagna was in the oven, I put together a salad and plated it, leaving enough room for the lasagna.

"I like watching you work," Cass remarked.

"Because it's more fun to watch people work than it is to do it yourself?" I joked.

He was a hard worker. He knew that, but I couldn't resist the dig.

He pushed his glasses back up his nose and pretended to look offended. "It's because you make it look so easy," he said. "But it's really not. It's like watching an artist paint a masterpiece."

"Their masterpieces last longer than mine do," I said.

I didn't mind putting in the work to produce something that took a few minutes to eat. I loved what I did. And I loved seeing people enjoy food. Even people like Getzoff.

"Yours tastes better," Cass replied.

"Oh?" I arched an eyebrow at him. "How many paintings have you eaten?"

He tipped his head back and burst out laughing, which was too fucking adorable.

"None," he said once he caught his breath, "I'll stick to eating actual food."

"And drinking milkshakes," I finished for him.

"That too," he added.

I pulled the lasagna out of the oven, sliced it carefully and placed it on the plate beside the salad.

Every so often I looked out at Getzoff, who seemed to be watching my customers while he waited for his meal.

Yeah, he definitely knew something.

# CHAPTER 10
## HARLOW

"Remember that time you said Fairfield's phone was too clean?" Boner clasped his hands in front of himself and slid a gaze in Cass' direction.

"Yeah?" Cass' brow crinkled.

Boner grunted. "This Getzoff guy. He's too clean."

"On paper, aren't you just as clean?" I asked.

"Not as clean as this bloke," Boner said. "I have a speeding ticket to my name. Maybe a drunk and disorderly."

"I'm shocked." Jules rolled his eyes.

"You are not shocked," Boner said.

Jules rolled his eyes harder. "Not even a little bit."

"That's better," Boner said approvingly. "Doesn't it feel good to be honest?"

Jules flipped him off with both middle fingers.

Boner grinned. "I'm starting to like this guy. Okay, *like* might be a strong word. I'm starting to not want to throw him in front of a subway train."

"Thanks," Jules said sarcastically. "I'm starting to not want to throw you in front of the Midtown bus. I won't rule out the Staten Island ferry."

"I have to admire a guy who has ambition," Boner said. "Getting me on that ferry, then off it again? That would be a feat of epic proportions.'"

"You don't like ferries?" I asked.

"Love, I don't like boats of any kind," he said. "Except rocking them." He pointed a finger gun at me. "That I can do."

"I've noticed that," I said with a smile. If anyone was good at rocking the boat, it was Boner.

"Is there a point to any of this?" Jules asked. "So he's clean. So what? How does that help us?"

"It means he's hiding something," Cass said, tapping his fingers against his lips thoughtfully. "Anyone who's hiding things has to hide them somewhere. We need to find said somewhere."

"Or we could stop looking," I suggested. "If we dig into him, he might return the favor."

"He's not going to find anything," Boner said confidently.

"You're sure about that?" I asked, not particularly certain myself.

"Of course, we're us, aren't we?" Boner said, unflinching. "We have mad skills between the five of us. And if we don't, Jules could find a way for him to accidentally electrocute himself."

"Jules could do that," Jules said reluctantly. "It's easier than you might think."

"Toaster in the bathtub," Boner suggested.

"That wouldn't be very subtle." Jules narrowed his eyes at the Englishman.

"No, but it'd be effective," Boner said. "Dibs on watching him zap." He threw his arms out to either side and shook his whole body like a sudden surge of deadly electricity was passing through him.

"You're an idiot," Jules told him.

Boner dropped his hands to his side. "Oh, care to enlighten us? How does someone look when they're being electrocuted?"

"Not like that," Jules said simply. "If you want a demonstration, I can throw a toaster into the bath the next time you're in there."

"That's *such* a generous offer," Boner said. "But I have to decline."

"Shame," Jules muttered.

"No one is going to fry anyone with a toaster," I said firmly.

"Of course not," Boner said. "Not when a hairdryer makes so much more sense. I mean, people would definitely think a toaster in the bathtub was suspicious."

"Unless someone likes to make toast while they bathe," Archer said.

"Is there anyone on the face of the planet who does that?" Boner seemed genuinely curious.

"Not that I'm aware of," Archer said, toying with the phone in his hand. "But if we can think up something, then someone's done it. It's like book genres. No matter how weird the idea you can come up with, someone's written it. Like snowman porn. Or deadly games of ping pong."

"What about dragon smut?" Boner challenged.

"It's a thing," Archer replied.

"Huh." Boner grunted. "What about door smut?"

"Also a thing," Archer said. "There's even a book about a self-service checkout."

Jules stared at him. "How do you even…" He shook his head. "You know what? Forget I asked. I don't want to know."

"You might learn something," Boner said, grinning at his expense. "What happens if one day you wake up as a self-serve checkout and you don't know how to fuck?"

"If I wake up one day as a self-serve checkout, fucking is going to be the last thing on my mind," Jules said.

"What will be the first?" Archer asked, his expression deadpan.

"Let me guess." Boner was having way too much fun with this. "The first thing you'd think about is how to weigh bananas."

"Have you had therapy recently?" Jules asked him. "Because you need therapy."

Boner laughed. "Is that denial I hear?" He placed a hand to his ear and listened intently.

"No, it's the sound of me telling you you're out of your fucking mind," Jules said darkly. After a moment, he added, "For the record, if I woke up tomorrow as a self-service checkout, I'd wonder how the hell I ended up that way. It'd probably be because of something Boner did."

"Guilty," Boner grinned. "If anyone could find a way to do that, it'd be me. Lucky for all of us, magic isn't a thing. We'll have to read books and imagine the possibilities."

"I wrote a fire hydrant romance once," Cass said, breaking the brief silence that followed Boner's words.

We all turned to look at him.

He shrugged. "They have long hoses."

I bit back a laugh.

"Can I read it someday?" I didn't want him to think I was making fun of him and his creativity. He piqued my curiosity, that was all.

"Yeah, I guess so," he said after a moment's hesitation. "You'll think it's weird."

"I want to know what happens when dogs piss on them," Boner said.

"Of course you do," Jules told him. "I bet that was your first thought when he mentioned fire hydrants." He didn't seem surprised to hear about his brother's writing. This might not be a revelation for him.

Boner spread his hands out to either side in a shrug. "Isn't that everyone's first thought when they think about a fire hydrant? I mean, they are famous for being pissed on by dogs. Am I right?"

He looked around at all of us.

"Yeah, you're right," I told him. "Cass might show us a new way to look at them. After all, they are useful for, you know, putting out fires."

Boner pretended to be shocked. "Is that what they're really for? I thought they were for dogs and street decoration."

Jules scooped up a spoon from beside his coffee cup and threw it in Boner's direction. It hit him on the chest, before bouncing off onto the floor. He grunted in annoyance. "I was aiming for his face."

"You missed." Boner smirked.

"No shit." If there was another spoon in front of him, Jules probably would have tried again. Instead, he finished his coffee and pushed his cup away, thankfully not using that as a projectile.

For one thing, it would hurt if it made contact with anyone, especially their face. For another thing, it might fall to the floor and break. I didn't think Archer would appreciate us breaking his cups without good reason.

What constituted a good reason? I could think of a few. Most involved Hypnos and Zeus.

"Now, where were we?" Boner pulled a chair out from the table, turned it around and sat on it backward.

"Snowman smut?" I suggested.

"No, before that." He scratched the side of his head. "Right, we were talking about Getzoff, and how suspiciously clean he is."

"What do you suggest we do about it? I asked. "We can't exactly stake out his place and wait for him to slip up. That would be suspicious. Not to mention time consuming. We need to focus on something else. Hypnos and Zeus are still out there."

"Yes, they are, and they're waiting for us to find them," Boner said.

"Let's stop obsessing about Detective Getzoff and focus on finding them." I turned to Cass. "Have you found anything new?"

He let out a long sigh. "I've looked through Fairfield's financials, as well as Solomon Danforth's financials. If they had any business partners in common, I couldn't find it. They didn't even use the same bank."

"That sounds suspicious to me." Boner said. "They were careful to keep everything separate. That's what I would do if I was an asshole like them."

Jules opened his mouth.

Cass gave him a slap on the chest with the back of his hand.

He closed it again.

They exchanged glares, but neither said anything.

"It could be suspicious and we could be barking up the wrong tree," I said reluctantly.

"They've been doing this for a long time," Archer said. "They know how to cover their tracks. We've always found them before. We'll find them this time."

"I hope so," I said softly. Sooner or later, something would turn up. A sign to tell us where to find them.

"Solomon said they weren't in the city," Jules pointed out. "They could be anywhere on the face of the planet."

"They could," I agreed. "But I don't think so."

"What are you basing that on?" Jules asked. He sounded accusing, but it was a reasonable question.

"Instinct," I said. I relied on it for a long time and

it never let me down. It wasn't going to let me down now.

"Harlow is right," Cass said. "I have the same feeling. They're here in the city somewhere."

"They might be in the next building," Boner said, his eyes shifting back and forth, like he was a cartoon character. "They could be on the other side of that wall right now." He pointed to his immediate left.

"That's the bathroom," I said.

"Right, well they could be that way." He pointed in the other direction.

"That's the outer wall. The street is on the other side," Archer said.

"They could be right below us then." Boner pointed down, giving us a look as if daring us to contradict him.

"They might be that close." I shivered. The idea made my stomach turn. If they were near the whole time, we could have dealt with them months ago. Years ago.

"Don't," Cass said. "Don't start thinking about things you think you should have done already."

He shot Jules a look, reminding him to keep his mouth shut before he could accuse me of not acting soon enough. He blamed me for what happened to his brother because I was busy setting up my restaurant. Because I hadn't tracked them down fast enough.

For a while, I thought he was right, but we'd hit a dead end with the last two on my list.

There was nothing I could do but carry on as normal. Keep working. Keep my restaurants open. Watch and wait.

"We will find them," Boner promised. "We'll find them and make them pay for the things they did. Then we'll make them pay a little bit more. Then just a tiny bit more." He held out his fingers slightly apart. "And when we're done with that, we'll make them wish they were never conceived."

"I wish they were never conceived," Cass said, glaring into his half-empty milkshake glass like he might find them there.

"Me too," I said with a sigh. "But they were, and we'll deal with them."

I wished I knew how, and where, if anywhere, Detective Getzoff fit into all of this.

What is it they say about tangled webs? I was starting to feel like I couldn't struggle out of this one. I'd come too far to stop now, but what if I never found them? What if the last two lines tattooed on my arm were never crossed off?

I had to accept the possibility Hypnos and Zeus might remain in the wind forever. For all I knew, they were dead already. If someone else was out there, doing the same things we were. If they'd killed Lionel Gammage, they might have gotten to them first.

This might all be for nothing.

My instincts told me it wasn't. They were out there. We just had to find them.

# CHAPTER 11
## HARLOW

startled wide awake when a hand clamped over my mouth.

"Shh," Archer whispered. "It's me."

He lifted his hand from my lips.

"What are you doing?" I whispered.

"I have a surprise for you. Come with me." He took my hand and helped me out of bed, leaving the covers to lie in a heap to the side.

He pulled me out into the living room and handed me a bundle of clothes: black jeans and a black sweater, a pair of black socks, and black shoes sat beside the door. He was already dressed the same.

"Get changed," he urged.

Blinking sleep out of my eyes, I did as he told me, stripping off my sleep pants and tank top and pulling on the black clothes.

"What are we doing?" I asked, as I pulled the sweater over my head.

"Wait and see," was all the response I was going to get from him, judging by the stony expression on his face.

"You know I don't like surprises," I told him.

"You're going to like this one," he said.

When I was fully dressed, he took my hand and led me out the door.

"We're not going to the apartment below this, are we?" I asked.

Boner had joked about our enemy being there, but I hadn't expected that to be literal.

"No, only old Mrs. Carboni lives there. And a couple of cats," Archer said. "She's harmless."

"They probably say that about me," I said dryly. "Except the part about having cats."

"Do you want a cat?" he asked, leading me down and out of the building.

"When would I have time to look after one?" I asked. I barely had enough time to look after myself these days, much less a pet.

"We'd all help if you wanted one," he said. "Statistically, it's much more difficult for a black cat to get adopted. One of those would be a perfect fit for you."

"Black like my heart," I told him.

He stopped mid-step and pulled me around to face him. "Your heart is anything but black." He pressed his mouth to mine, soft and reassuring.

"There are a bunch of souls in hell that would disagree with you," I said, but I kissed him back.

Reluctantly he drew away and resumed walking, his fingers laced in mine.

"It's not far," he said. "Just around the corner."

"Do the others know about this?" I asked.

"No, I decided to keep this between us," he said. "I missed doing this alone with you." He squeezed my hand.

"Is that the only reason?" I asked. "It doesn't have anything to do with you not trusting them. Do you think one of them snuck ahead and killed Lionel Gammage before we got there?"

"We were all together for that," he said. "None of them could have snuck ahead. They could have called ahead to someone else though." He chewed on that thought for a moment.

"So you don't trust them." I didn't know how I felt about that. I had feelings for all four of them. That didn't automatically mean they had to like each other. I mean, it would help if they did, but the situation was complicated at best.

"I trust you and myself," he said. "I *want* to trust

them." He put the slightest emphasis on the word. "I know you do."

"Yeah, I do," I said, brushing hair back off my face. "But I've misplaced my trust before."

"Your trust in me isn't misplaced," he assured me. "I'd never do anything to hurt you or betray you. I know I'm not the most…normal person. People think I'm strange."

He exhaled out his nose. "I don't give a shit what they think. I only care what you think."

"I don't think you're strange," I told him. "You're unique. I like that about you. It makes you special."

"I don't think anyone's ever called me special in a nice way before," he said. "Here." He handed me a mask and put one over his own face. I gave him a smile before disappearing behind the hard, black plastic.

We walked on for a while before he stopped in front of a store. It was quiet at this time of night. Or morning, to be exact.

I looked inside my heart fluttering with nerves. "There's got to be all sorts of cameras."

"There are," he agreed. "I was down here earlier checking the place out."

"Then what?" The idea of being caught on camera put me on edge. We didn't take risks like that.

"Trust me." Still holding my hand, he led me into the store.

This looked like every other convenience store in the country. A display of Doritos off to the side. A fridge full of soda and water. A shelf with a couple of half-blackened bananas and sad-looking apples.

Further back was a counter with a cash register. Behind it stood a woman a few years younger than me. She took one look at us and our clothes and her eyes widened in fear.

"We're not here to rob you," Archer said. "We're looking for Toby."

Her throat bobbed as she swallowed. She nodded and jerked her head toward the back of the store.

"In the storeroom," she said in a whisper. Absently, she rubbed at a bruise on her arm.

Archer nodded and led me to the back, moving slowly, silently.

"Please," the young woman whispered behind us. "Make it hurt."

Archer glanced back and nodded back. "We will."

We stepped into the storeroom to find a man sitting on a box, his phone in his hand. His cock in the other.

"Yeah, just like that," he said to the video he was watching. "Hurt her good."

Was that… Ugh, sick. People like him made my skin crawl.

He caught a hint of movement in the corner of his eye and looked up to see us. He startled so violently he almost lost his grip on the phone. Hastily he tucked his cock back into his pants.

"What the fuck?"

"Toby Dent?" Archer asked, his voice menacing behind his mask.

"Yes," Toby started to say. "I mean, no. Never heard of the guy."

"You're a really bad liar," I told him. "Like, really bad."

He pushed himself to his feet. He was tall, but carrying a few extra pounds. Sweat glistened on his brow. The smell of fear wafted from him. Or maybe he hadn't showered in a day or two. Either way, it was unpleasant.

"We know about the things you got up to," Archer said. "With young women who didn't consent."

"What the hell? I'd never do anything like that. Ask Camilla." He looked around us in the direction of the young woman although he couldn't have seen her from where he stood.

"I did ask her," Archer said. "She told us to make it hurt."

"That little bitch," Toby, snarled. "I knew I should

have whipped her ass hard—" He stopped mid-sentence, realizing he condemned himself.

"She deserved it," he said changing tack, like all abusers did. Blaming the victim for the things they did to them.

"We both know that's not true. I said. "No one deserves that."

"He does," Archer pointed out.

"Right, he does," I agreed. "But she doesn't."

"What do you want?" Toby asked, backing up a few steps until his back hit a shelf.

"We want world peace, free chocolate, and no sexual predators," I said.

Not necessarily in that order.

Toby frowned, confused. "I can give you free fucking chocolate. You can have all the chocolate you want," he gestured wildly toward a shelf full of boxes.

"You stock Cadbury chocolate?" I asked. "If I knew that, I might have come in here sooner."

"Of course I do," he said almost looking proud of the fact, as if somehow that made up for everything else he'd done in life. Chocolate was good, but not *that* good.

"Do you have a will?" Archer asked.

"What?" Now Toby frowned at him. "What do I need a will for?"

Archer pulled out his knife and took a step forward. "Because someone is about to inherit this place."

"What the fuck? No." Toby tried to back up further, but there was nowhere to go. "You really want to do this to Camilla? I'm the only parent she has left."

"Camilla will be just fine," I said coldly.

I'd make sure of that. She'd probably run this place better than him. If she stocked Cadbury chocolate, I was happy to frequent the place. Probably too often.

Toby reached around behind him, trying to find something to fight back with. He put his hand on a box and pulled it forward, dipping his fingers inside. He grabbed out the first thing he touched and pulled it out as if it was some kind of weapon.

"Nacho cheese Doritos," Archer remarked.

I could hear the smirk in his voice.

"Well, I'm scared," I said sarcastically. "Death by nachos."

"There's worse ways to die than eating too many nachos," Archer said.

"Absolutely," I agreed.

Toby threw away the packet in disgust and tried to find something else.

He grabbed up a ketchup bottle. Desperate, he

twisted it open and aimed it at Archer's mask. With both hands, he squeezed, squirting the condiment in the direction of Archer's eyes.

Archer turned his face and caught the ketchup on the side of his head instead. It hit with a splat and trickled down his clothes, leaving a red smear.

"Is that the best you've got?" I asked, trying to contain a laugh. "Maybe you could add some mustard."

"Maybe you could fuck off." Toby threw the bottle at me, aiming for my head.

I ducked.

Archer lunged, and jammed the knife into Toby's throat.

*"No one throws a ketchup bottle at my woman."*

While Toby gurgled, drowning in his own blood, Archer twisted the knife, driving it in deeper.

"No mustard for us, I suppose," I said, pretending to be sad about it.

"Next time." Archer yanked the knife back.

Blood spurted out of Toby's neck. He sank to his knees, then fell backwards against one of the shelves. They rattled. Boxes of cereal wobbled.

A single box of cornflakes at the front wobbled more violently before toppling forward and landing on Toby's leg.

A moment later, the shelves gave way, soda cans

raining down on him. Boxes containing deodorant, condoms, and tampons followed, piling up over and around him, like the whole store had been upended.

"Now you've made a mess," Archer said, sounding irritated. "Camilla's not going to appreciate having to clean that up."

"It looks like these shelves were put up badly anyway," I remarked. "She can have them done properly."

Unless, of course, she decided to sell the place. No doubt it held a bunch of disturbing memories. Sometimes it was better to get away and move on with life, than to stay in places that bring us pain.

For half a second I contemplated buying the store myself. Almost as quickly, I dismissed the idea. I had enough on my plate with two restaurants. What would I do with a convenience store?

"Bad workmanship," Archer grumbled. He put his knife away, snagged up a chocolate bar and handed it to me. "We should get out of here."

"Yes, we should." I followed him out of the storeroom.

Camilla was still behind the checkout.

"Sorry about the mess," I told her.

"That's okay," she whispered. "I've been trying to get him to do something about those shelves for a long time. They were bound to fall and kill someone sooner or later."

"Yes, they were," I agreed.

If they looked closely, they'd see a gaping hole in his neck. Who knows, maybe they'd accept the death by shelves excuse. After all, if we hadn't killed him, they would have. Right?

Archer took my hand and we stepped back out into the night.

# CHAPTER 12
## ARCHER

"That was fun," Harlow said as we stepped back into my apartment.

"It was. You've got a bit of…" I swiped chocolate off the side of her mouth with my thumb before pressing it between my lips. "Yum." She had a point about Cadbury chocolate.

She let me take her hand and lead her over to the bathroom, where I started the bath. With water, not acid.

"I figured we could clean up together," I said, working my hand under the hem of her sweater to pull it up over her head. She held up her arms to help me, then pulled mine up and off.

"Good idea. You have ketchup in your hair and on your ear."

I put my hand up to feel it. My hair was stiff, and the side of my head was sticky.

I grunted in disgust. I didn't like being dirty, much less sticky. What was the point of stickiness anyway? Why did the universe need things to stick? Okay, tape and envelopes, but those were a different kind of sticky. Those were sticky with a purpose.

This was sticky to gross me out.

The rest of my clothes were caked with the condiment. I stripped them off and threw them aside. They'd need a good wash after I had one.

I turned off the water and threw in some bath salts. The scented steam rose off the water, filling the room with smells that were better than sticky ketchup.

I helped Harlow into the bath, then climbed in myself, sitting opposite her, my feet on either side of her hips.

"I call this a good night," I said. "One killing and one bath with my woman."

"The perfect date," she said.

"Almost perfect." I grabbed a washcloth and started to wipe the ketchup off my ear. "I wasn't able to get you his heart."

"He was a little bit busy under all of those cans and boxes," she said with a laugh. "I can live without his heart."

"Are you sure?" I dug the washcloth into the space behind my ear and scrubbed up and down vigorously.

"Very sure," she said. "It's sweet of you to be worried about me though."

"I'm a big believer in supporting people's hobbies," I said.

"Collecting human hearts. Is that a hobby now?" she asked with a small husky laugh.

The sound went straight to my cock.

"If it's your hobby, then it's a hobby," I said. "Besides, it's my way of telling you that you have mine."

"That's so sweet," she said, cocking her head at me and letting the tips of her hair fall into the water. "I prefer your heart right where it is." She leaned forward and pressed her hand to my chest.

My heart thumped harder at her touch.

"Me too." I looked down at her hand. "I'm kinda attached to it. Not to mention, outside of heart transplants, one hundred percent of people who are missing a physical, biological heart can't live without it."

"I believe that statistic," she said, stroking a hand over my chest and down to my abs. "Although I know a few people who seem to have figured out how to live without a brain."

I snorted. My equivalent of a loud laugh. "Anyone I know?

"Possibly," she said. "You might move in the same circles as some of them."

"As long as you're not accusing me of living without a brain." I kept my expression and tone deadpan, but I was laughing on the inside.

I'd kept my emotions in check ever since I could remember. It was easier than responding in a way people considered 'incorrect.' Laughing when I shouldn't laugh. Being angry at things I shouldn't be angry at. How was a guy supposed to get it right every time?

Besides, if you deadpan a joke and no one laughs, you're not losing, right?

"I would never," she assured me. Her hand wandered down lower, grazing my stomach just above my rapidly growing cock. "You're one of the smartest people I know."

"Does that say a lot about them, or about me?" I said, teasing again.

She laughed. "It's definitely about you. You're quick, clever and hot as hell."

Her thumb brushed the head of my cock, making it twitch and leap to attention.

"No one's ever called me hot as hell before." Not

even hotter than heck. Not even hot at all, that I was aware of.

"Remind me to find out where Cass got his glasses," she said. "I can pass their details on to… I don't know, everyone else. They need their eyes checked if they don't see how hot you are."

"You're going to make me blush." Her thumb stroked the side of my cock. If she kept doing that, I was going to do more than blush. I was going to come right here in the bath water.

"You know what? I don't care what anyone else thinks," I said. "Only you."

Her opinion meant everything to me.

"I definitely think that." She curled her hand around my length, stroking slowly and gently, like she had all night.

"You're the hot one here," I whispered, trying not to pump myself into her hand. "Sometimes I think I'm dreaming. I pinch myself but then you're still here. Maybe I'm having some crazy hallucination."

"No hallucination." She let go of my cock and scooted forward, until her legs draped over my thighs. She placed her hands on my shoulders and positioned her pussy against the tip of my cock.

"If this wasn't real, would you feel this?" She lowered herself onto me slowly, inch by inch.

"If this is a hallucination, I don't want a cure." I

bracketed her hips with my hands and half-closed my eyes. "You feel so fucking good."

Her pussy had my cock in a vise, her heat clamping down on me like she might never let go. I didn't want her to let go. I could have sat here like this with her forever, maybe beyond forever, doing this with her.

At this exact moment, it felt like we'd done this before in multiple past lives. I didn't care. What mattered right now was…right now. Right here.

"You feel incredible," I whispered.

"So do you," she whispered back.

Using my shoulders for leverage, she raised herself up, half-pulling off me before sliding back down.

I thrust up into her a few times, the water splashing against the side of the bath and threatening to go over onto the floor.

I leaned forward and took one of her nipples in my mouth, sucking gently before switching to the other one, tasting her warm, bath salt-scented skin.

Forget chocolate, nothing tasted better than this woman.

I pressed a hand between us, stroking her clit with my fingers while we rolled our hips. Creating the only kind of friction I liked.

She moaned softly. Her hips shifting, seeking my

hand. Needing more. I watched her face, listened to her breaths. Paid attention when I hit the right spot. Then working her. Right there. A little harder. A little faster. A little more.

"Archer," she whispered. "Oh god, I'm going to… Going to come." She was breathless now. Moaning and writhing against my fingers.

"Come for me," I said softly.

Watching her break apart in front of me and around me was a bigger high than killing. A bigger high than coming myself, which I did a few moments after her. Her pussy tight around me, drawing an orgasm out of me. I couldn't have resisted if I tried.

Which I didn't. Because why would I resist coming inside this incredible woman?

My release exploded inside her. Surrounding my cock with extra heat and wetness. Drowning me. I might have died inside her for a moment or two. Died happy.

And then we were sagging together. Holding each other. Breathing heavily.

"The perfect date," she whispered.

"The perfect woman," I whispered back.

She laughed softly, her chest vibrating against mine.

"Don't say you're not," I said before she could

respond. "To kill with and then have a bath with after, you're perfect."

There was no one else I'd rather do any of this with. Harlow was it for me. If anything happened to her, there'd never be anyone else.

She might as well put my heart in a jar right now, because all of it belonged to her. Every fiber. Every drop of blood.

"I love you," I said softly, stroking her damp hair.

"I love you too," she said back.

Reluctantly, I eased her off my cock and turned her around to reach for the shampoo bottle. If I was good at anything, it was cleaning. I wanted to wash every inch of her.

I started with her hair, then her body. Rubbing body wash into her shoulders to ease the tension. Then working my way down slowly.

"Turn around," I said so I could reach her legs and her feet, massaging down between her toes until she started to look sleepy.

"Mmm," she hummed, closing her eyes. "You have magic hands."

"You have magic everything," I told her. Boner was wrong. Magic did exist. She was proof of it.

She opened one eye and smiled at me.

"Everything," I said firmly, massaging the ball of

her foot. "Magic smile. Magic nipples. Magic pussy." I shrugged one shoulder. "I'm just saying."

"Archer Hardwick, you're such a romantic," she said, smiling softly.

"Only when it comes to you," I told her. She was turning me into a big puddle of goo, and I wasn't even mad about it. I wasn't usually a big fan of goo of any kind, but I'd wear the title if she gave it to me.

Archer Goo Hardwick didn't roll off the tongue, but whatever.

"Turn around again," I told her.

I pressed her down gently so her hair was under the water and rinsed off the conditioner, massaging her scalp and washing off every last drop of the stuff.

I didn't want to leave a trace of chemicals in her hair. What sort of boyfriend would I be if I did that?

She stifled a yawn with her fist as I was finishing.

I gently squeezed the excess water out of her hair, then helped her out of the bath and dried her off carefully, making sure to pat her everywhere.

"Thank you," she said, holding up her arm so I could dry under there. "I'm not sure if I deserve all of this attention."

I stopped and looked up at her sharply. "You deserve all of this and more. If I could, I'd spend the rest of my life spoiling you rotten, starting with regular deliveries of Cadbury chocolate right to the front door."

"Now you really are spoiling me," she said with a laugh. "Boner would probably eat it before I got to it."

"I'm not above killing him so you can have the chocolate," I said dryly.

I liked the guy, but if she wanted me to kill him, I would. Same with Cass and Jules. I wouldn't like it, but I'd do it.

"Don't go killing Boner, or any of them," she said firmly. "We can always get more chocolate."

"Yes, we can," I said. "Maybe chocolate sauce next time."

She smiled. "I'd like that."

I was hoping she'd say that because I'd like it too. I'd cover her with as much of it as I could and lick it all off, slowly and carefully, until she was completely, perfectly clean.

I startled as the bathroom door opened behind me. Boner stood there, his face red.

"Where the hell were you two?"

# CHAPTER 13
## HARLOW

"Are you two out of your minds?" Jules snarled.

He sat in one of the dining chairs, his legs apart, wearing only a pair of boxer shorts.

I didn't expect him to sleep in shorts covered in pictures of cute frogs, but here we were.

"That police detective is sniffing around, and you go out there and kill someone?" He was all but shouting the words at us.

"Do you want the whole city to hear?" I snapped.

"No. It seems like you do," he retorted. "Whose stupid idea was it anyway?"

"It wasn't a stupid idea and it was mine," Archer said coolly.

Jules shook his head. "I thought you were smarter

than that, bro."

"They weren't caught," Cass pointed out.

Jules rounded on him. "Are you sure about that? Are you sure they weren't seen? They could have been followed. They could have brought him here. He could be standing outside the fucking door right now." He waved a fist toward the door.

"Listening to every word you're saying," Boner said to Jules, although he looked as irritated about us sneaking away in the middle of the night.

Jules looked like he was going to tell Boner to fuck off, but he closed his mouth. When he spoke again, it was quieter by a fraction of a decibel.

"It was a stupid risk."

"We were seen. The place has cameras and there was a witness. But she's not going to say anything," Archer said.

"There was a—" Jules stared at him. "Now I know you're out of your ever-loving fucking mind. You can't know she won't say anything."

"He's right," I said.

"Of course I am," Jules snapped.

"I was referring to Archer," I said calmly, "She's not going to say anything. She was grateful for our help."

"For now," Jules reasoned. "What happens when she decides she's not so grateful after all? What happens when she decides you've made her life worse? She has camera footage."

Cass rose, headed over to pick up his laptop and opened it. He sat tapping at the screen for a few minutes, then shook his head. "Not anymore. I wiped it clean."

"Too clean?" Jules asked, no less pissed off. "They left an eyewitness."

"Who saw two people dressed in black with masks," I said. "She can't give anything to the police even if she wanted to."

"Two people in masks and one is a woman," Jules pointed out. "That's something, whether you want to believe it or not. Getzoff is already suspicious of you."

"Why didn't you tell us you were going out?" Boner asked, sounding hurt.

"We were on a date," Archer said. "I wanted some time alone with Harlow."

"Okay, but why didn't you tell us?" Boner insisted. "I woke up and Harlow was gone. I heard you come back. Figured you'd explain. But no, you went and had a bath." He gestured toward the bathroom.

"Archer had ketchup in his ear," I said.

Boner dropped his hand. "In his hair, ear," he repeated. "You didn't think I'd want to see that?" His anger was starting to fade, replaced by his usual humor.

"It was sticky," Archer said, curling his lip slightly. His version of being completely grossed out.

"You got sticky and I missed it?" Boner flopped down into a chair, exhaling as he hit the seat.

"It wasn't a good kind of sticky," I told him. "That didn't happen until we got home."

"I heard the water sloshing," he said, looking down at the tabletop in front of him.

"Are you disappointed because you missed the killing, or because we didn't tell you before we left?" I asked.

He raised his hands in front of him and moved them up and down, like a set of scales. "A little of this and a little of that. You two had fun, by the sound of it."

"We did," I agreed. "Next time you and I can have fun together."

"You really are out of your minds," Jules said, his arms crossed over his bare chest. "I thought the idea was to keep an eye on Getzoff and keep a low profile. Killing convenience store owners isn't what I'd call 'keeping a low profile.'" He used air quotes. "And leaving a witness?"

"Do you want us to go back and kill her? She's innocent," I snapped. "He was hurting her."

"She tried to get help," Archer said softly. "No one would listen until we did."

Silence followed his words.

We knew it happened all too often. People reached out for support and didn't receive it. No part of that was okay. We shouldn't have needed it to do what we did tonight. If the system worked, we wouldn't have. Sometimes it let people like Camilla down, and here we were. Taking care of the problem instead.

Jules scrubbed a hand over his face. "Okay, I get it. No one listened when Augustus needed help either. They gave him no choice but to…"

He closed his eyes without finishing the sentence. He didn't need to, we knew what he was going to say. The system let Augustus down too.

"Did you have to do it where you'd be seen?" Jules asked finally.

"They had an apartment above the convenience store," Archer said. "It was harder to get in there than it was to do it directly. Either way, she would have been there. Either way, he'd end up dead. I promise you, I was as careful as I could possibly be."

"That still doesn't explain why you didn't tell us you were leaving," Boner said. Apparently he was more worried about that than he was about us being seen.

"I thought you'd try to talk us out of it, or tag along," Archer said. "Next time I'll leave a note."

"Do that," Boner said. "Look, I understand wanting to have time alone with Harlow. Just give us a heads up, yeah? And I'll do the same for the rest of you."

I rubbed a hand over my eyes.

"Is there anything else? Because I need to get some rest. I have to be at work in a few hours."

I was going to be tired all day but it was worth it seeing the gratitude on Camilla's face. Toby was the lowest of the low. I hoped that special place in hell for people like him had an extra special spot for him. Something painful.

Strange how I always thought that when I didn't really believe in heaven or hell. Thinking of predators dying without any kind of retribution didn't sit well with me. That was why I had my torture box. For a chosen few, I could ensure they suffered before they died. If they didn't suffer after they died, at least they had that.

"So do I," Jules muttered. He pushed himself off the chair and stalked over to his bedroom. The bed creaked as he threw himself down onto it and rolled over.

"Sorry about him, but he does have a point," Cass

said, closing the laptop and sitting in the chair Jules vacated. "That was a risk."

"Calculated risk," Archer said. "Carefully calculated." His tone was loaded with additional meaning.

Cass cocked his head. "What did you do?"

We all turned to stare at Archer.

"I figured if the cops knew she was a woman, they might give her a fancy nickname," he admitted. "They call me the Heart-Renderer. Isn't it time she got one of her own?"

I groaned. "If they look that place over carefully enough, I might get the nickname The Ketchup Killer."

Boner grinned. "That's fucking hilarious. Harlow, The Ketchup Killer."

"They might call you the Chocolate Killer," Archer suggested.

"That sounds like I killed chocolate," I grumbled.

Which was more or less accurate. Okay, not killing it, but eating it.

"They might not realize he was murdered," Boner said. "They might put it down to..." He paused for dramatic effect. "Shelf-inflicted injuries."

We all groaned at his terrible pun.

As always, he was completely unapologetic. He actually bowed.

"Thank you, I do what I *can*," he said.

"Shut up with the puns," Jules called out.

"No *can* do," Boner called back. "It goes with the rest of my evil personality, as a…cereal killer."

"They might call me the Cornflake Killer," I said, remembering the box that fell off the shelf. That would be a play on the term serial killer.

"They might go for something sophisticated, if they know he was a predator," Archer said slowly. "Something like the Feminine Hygienist." The very corners of his mouth twitched upward.

"If you don't stop with the puns, I'm going to kill all of you myself," Jules said.

"You might not need to," I called back. "I might do it for you."

To Archer I said, "I hope they come up with something better than that. But they're not going to call me Chef Stabby based on what we did tonight."

That disappointed me more than I would have expected it to. I mean, the nickname I gave myself was cute, right?

"Why don't you kill with a big carving knife?" Boner asked. "Or a vegetable peeler?"

"It's harder to conceal a carving knife," I pointed out. "And a vegetable peeler would be as effective as killing someone with a wooden spoon."

"You could totally kill someone with a wooden spoon, love," he said. "It'll take a while, but it's possible. Although, if you jam it down their throat, that'll be faster." He mimed doing just that, jabbing a spoon with both of his hands down the throat of an imaginary adversary.

"Thank you for not suggesting I stick it up their ass," I said.

I wouldn't do that to a perfectly good wooden spoon. Not to mention there were parts of these predators I didn't want to go near if I could help it. They were assholes. I didn't want to touch their assholes. You know what they say about those. Everyone has one. That doesn't mean everyone wants to see them.

"I have a friend in Dusk Bay who likes to torture people with a vegetable peeler," Archer said.

We all turned to stare at him.

"Sounds like you know some interesting people," Boner remarked. "Maybe you could introduce me sometime."

"I think he'd like you," Archer said. "He's even more unhinged than you are."

"Take that back," Boner said, waggling his finger at Archer. "No one is more unhinged than I am."

"Believe me, he is," Archer said. "Harlow's torture box and my acid bath? They'd be child's play to this guy."

"Now I'm not just curious, I'm a little bit turned on," Boner said.

"Just when I think I've heard everything," Cass said softly. "You surprise me. All of you." He sighed.

I leaned over to wrap my arm around his shoulders.

"I feel like we've corrupted an innocent person. I should have said no when you started to get involved with all of this."

"You tried," he reminded me. "I was the one who got myself involved. It's just… The world is more fucked up than I thought it was. Which is saying something, because I had some idea."

Boner barked a laugh. "No offense, bro, but you have no idea how fucked up it really is out there. Trust me."

Archer hummed his agreement.

Cass leaned into me. "Promise me if you go anywhere to do what you did tonight, you'll let me know first."

He sounded tired, but he injected a hint of his bedroom dominance into the last few words, making certain I heard and understood.

"Promise," I whispered. "No more going off without letting you all know."

"That's all we ask," Cass said. "When Boner said you were missing, I assumed the worst."

I squeezed his shoulders. "We didn't mean to worry you."

"We worry because we love you," Boner said.

"Exactly," Cass agreed. "We were ready to burn the world down to find you."

"I'm right here," I told him. "I'm not going anywhere."

I never had people worried for me like this before. This was a promise I wouldn't break.

# CHAPTER 14
## HARLOW

"Toby's death was ruled accidental," Cass said, looking up from his laptop to give me an apologetic look.

"Good," Jules said, scowling at both of us over the top of his cornflakes. "They might not come after any of us."

"That's rude," Boner said, scraping a heap of peanut butter over a slice of toast. "All that effort Archer went to so they'd notice Harlow and give her a nickname, and they put it down to what? Death by sardine can?"

Archer sighed softly.

"It doesn't say," Cass said. "Just that shelves fell on him and he died. Along with a warning to make sure shelves are put up correctly."

"Good, some practical advice." Boner stabbed the

knife into the toast at an angle, cutting it into two rough triangles.

"You comprehend none of that is as important as the fact they aren't looking for a murderer or two?" Jules said. Where once he would have looked around at us in disbelief, this morning he looked resigned. Like he was starting to understand our collective sense of humor, even when it seemed our priorities were inside out.

"That's a good thing," Archer said. He didn't seem convinced.

"We can find someone else to go after," I assured him. "There's plenty more bad apples where Toby came from."

"I know." He paused for a moment before nodding to himself. "I'll find someone. We can do it better this time. Make sure to take their heart out. Or…something."

"You definitely need an 'or something,'" Boner said. "Otherwise they'll think it's you, not her."

"What about you?" Jules asked, pointing his spoon at Boner. "Don't you want some nickname they'll put in serial killer documentaries in a few years?"

Boner shrugged. "Of course I do. But not before Harlow gets one. She's been working her cute little ass off for years. She deserves to be recognized. And by recognized, I mean given a cute nickname. Not *literally* recognized."

"We figured you meant that," I told him.

"Speak for yourself," Jules said. "Who knows when it comes to this guy?" He prodded the air in Boner's direction before finishing his cereal.

Boner made kissy faces at Jules before chomping down on his toast and chewing.

Jules responded with an eye roll.

"As much fun as this is," I said finishing the last of my coffee, "I need to get to work."

"Me too," Cass said. He closed his laptop and rose to his feet. "I wouldn't want to be late. I might get in trouble with the boss." He gave me a grin that made my stomach flip.

"Your boss might enjoy that," I teased.

He shoved hair back off his face as his cheeks turned pink. For a moment he looked like he was going to order me onto my knees and punish my mouth with his cock. Then he glanced at his watch and saw we really would be late if we didn't get out the door soon.

"Later," I told him.

I placed my cup in the dishwasher, brushed my teeth and grabbed my things. By the time I was ready to head out the door, so was everyone else, including Archer, who looked like he hadn't slept at all.

"I don't need a big escort," I told them all.

"I'm leaving now anyway," Jules said. He picked up his tools that were in a box by the door and stomped out ahead of us.

"I like escorting you," Boner said. He hooked his elbow around mine.

"Me too," Archer agreed. "It's a nice morning for a walk."

"It's raining," I pointed out.

"A little bit of moisture never hurt anyone," Boner said. "Unless it's acid. Or a bunch of other shit that actually would hurt. A whole lot of water can hurt you too." He chuckled.

Archer snagged an umbrella from the hall table and followed us out.

"You know why they say you shouldn't open those inside?" Boner asked.

"It's bad luck," Cass suggested.

"It's bad luck because you can poke someone's eye out," Boner said. He pulled out an umbrella of his own and opened it once we were out on the street, making sure half of it was covering my head.

Cass and Archer huddled under the other one.

"I love this place when it rains," Boner started to say.

He stopped when a cab flew past us, flinging up water onto the curb and drenching all down one side of him. "Did I mention I hate rain?" He shook his leg out, trying to dry it, but he was holding back a smile. It would take more than a bit of water to upset Edward Bonegard.

"Look on the bright side. You standing there kept me dry," I said with a grin.

"Of course I did," Boner sniffed. "That's why I put myself here. What sort of gentleman would I be if I let you get wet?" He stopped for a moment. "On the outside. A gentleman makes absolutely sure to get his woman wet on the *inside*." He winked at me, then drew me down the street toward Angel's Rest.

"We have a new artist on display at the gallery," he said as we walked. "You should come and check it out after your lunch shift. He's very talented."

"As talented as you?" I asked.

"At art, yes," Boner said. "At other things, definitely not."

"You seem very sure of that," I pointed out.

No doubt he was right, but if we couldn't joke around with each other, where was the fun in our relationship?

"A guy has to be confident about some things," Boner said. "Especially if he's going to go by the nickname of Boner. That leaves me a lot to live up to, wouldn't you say? Besides, I know you enjoy yourself. Cass too."

I glanced back at Cass. His head was tilted at an angle, trying to stay under the other umbrella. At the same time he was trying to walk at the same speed as Archer, who seemed in a hurry this morning.

"I don't think Cass is complaining either," I agreed, giving him a soft smile.

"Only about the rain," Cass said. "I'm used to it where I come from."

"Funny," Boner smirked. "I was going to say the same thing. You know what they say about rainy old London."

"What is it they say?" I asked.

He grinned. "That it's rainy and old."

I snorted a laugh. "Yeah, that is what people say, isn't it?" I'd never been there so I couldn't say if it was true or not. I guessed it was, since people said it often enough.

"Have you ever thought about living somewhere it doesn't rain all the time?" I asked.

"Like the desert? Hell no," he said. "The last thing I want is sandy balls. Between you and me, I'm not a big fan of beaches either, for the same reason. No one likes a sandy asscrack."

He nodded at a couple of older women who walked by as he said that. They looked at him like he was out of his mind, and hurried on.

"They must be new to the city," he remarked,

watching them for a moment before turning back the way we were headed.

"If you shocked them, they're definitely in for an interesting time," I said.

"Right?" He smiled slowly. "I'm not that shocking." His blue eyes shined and he held back a grin.

"You're very shocking but it's one of the things I love about you," I told him. "You always keep things interesting around here."

"Thank fuuuck for that," he drawled. "I'd hate if you were bored with me around. Life is way too short to be bored." After a beat, he added, "Depending on the circumstances. Sometimes a little bit of boredom is required. Right, Hardy?

"Hardwick," Archer responded. "But yes, sometimes, boredom has to happen. I prefer to think of it as patience."

"You make a good point," Boner said. "There is a fine line between boredom and patience. Especially in our line of work. And by work I mean..." He trailed off and glanced around.

"We know what you mean," I said quickly. "I'm sure you're never bored at the gallery."

"I'm usually too busy to be bored," he agreed. "Like you at the restaurant. There's always something going on. Something that needs doing. Something that needs to be cleaned up off the floor. Did I tell you about the time someone dropped a squid on the floor?"

"A squid?" I asked. Maybe I shouldn't take the bait, but he had me curious. I mean, what was a squid doing in a gallery?

"An actual squid," Boner said. "It wasn't alive. The guy thought it could be a new type of art installation. You know, place it on the floor. Position its tentacles and voila, art."

"You didn't agree?" I asked.

"Oh no, I agreed," Boner said. "It looked amazing, but it smelt like shit. Had to ask the guy to remove it. It took some cleaning to get the smell to go away."

"What happened to the artist?" I asked.

He rubbed his chin thoughtfully. "I never heard from him again. I think he decided on another angle, something less pungent."

"Sounds like it would have worked better at my restaurant on a plate, not on the floor in the gallery," I said.

He snapped his fingers, "You're right. If I knew you then, I would have sent him to you instead. That squid would have made a nice lunch."

"You lead an interesting life," I told him. "I bet you get all sorts of strange people at the gallery."

"Some days I'm not the strangest one there," he

agreed. "I bet Archer has all sorts of stories like that. Peculiar people in a theater or movie studio?"

"A few," Archer agreed. "Usually it's people telling me I should turn their life story into a screenplay."

"Have you ever done that?" I asked, trying to keep an eye on the direction we were walking while glancing over my shoulder.

"No," he said with a half-shrug. "I tell them they should write it themselves."

"Do they?" Boner asked.

"Not that I know of," Archer said. "It's possible they try, but discover, writing is harder than they think."

"Is that true, Cass?" Boner asked, another grin playing at the corners of his mouth. "How difficult is it to write fire hydrant smut?"

"Very difficult," Cass agreed. "More than I expected."

"Approximately three percent of the population ever write and complete a manuscript," Archer said. "The percentage of people who want to do it is much higher. Well done for finishing yours."

"Thank you," Cass said, looking surprised. I got the impression he'd never given it much thought beyond actually writing the story. Archer was right, though. Getting it down on paper, or on screen, was a big achievement.

"When do we get to read it then?" Boner asked. "Don't think I'm going to forget."

"I don't know," Cass said. "It's not very good." He was visibly relieved when we arrived at the restaurant.

I unlocked the door and we hurried inside, out of the rain, the topic of fire hydrant smut forgotten for now.

# CHAPTER 15

## HARLOW

You know the exact moment you think everything has been too quiet and then things blow up in your face?

I saw no sign of Detective Getzoff for four days. I almost started to forget he existed when he walked into my restaurant, almost at the end of the dinner service.

I caught a glimpse of him as I was putting the finishing touches to a couple of desserts.

I muttered something under my breath.

"Are you okay?" Cass asked, stepping over and peering out in a very non-inconspicuous way. "Oh."

"Yeah, oh," I said, tidying up the plates and sliding in a couple of spoons.

I handed them over to Shelly, who hurried away with them.

"Chef St. James." Getzoff strode over to the kitchen like he owned the place. "Looks like you have a busy night here."

I glanced up at him as I grabbed another couple of bowls and started spooning dessert into them.

"Very busy. Have you come for more of the lasagna?" I asked. "Or maybe I could tempt you with dessert?"

I ignored Cass' glance at my face at the use of the word 'tempt.' He should know by now I was only offering food. This man didn't interest me in any way, except curiosity at why he kept lurking around.

"That does look good," he agreed. "I thought I'd come and see how you are. With all the goings on in the neighborhood."

"Goings on?" I looked up at him with one eye.

"Yes, there's been some unfortunate accidents in the local area over the last few weeks, possibly even months."

"With this amount of people in a small radius, you're going to get accidents," I said. I flashed him a slight smile before returning my attention to the dessert.

There was an increase in unexplained disappearances and the occasional murder since I started committing them, but I was careful to spread them out, knowing at some point the police would start looking for a pattern.

"That's true," he agreed. "But some are more suspicious than others."

"I'm sure they are." I put spoons into the next round of desserts and placed them up for Shelly to take to customers.

"I understand one of your staff was murdered right here in this restaurant," he said, looking around at the seating area as if somehow it would reveal blood that was spilt here.

I washed my hands and wiped them slowly on a towel. "That's right. The police are still looking for her killer."

"And you're still operating a restaurant here," he observed.

"A girl has to make a living," I said, making sure to add the right amount of regret to my tone. I didn't need to fake it. I still missed Erin. I hated what Gina did to her, but she of all people wouldn't have wanted me to close the restaurant because of it.

She knew the importance of the people I was helping here, and the money I donated to shelters from the profits. She wouldn't have wanted her death to be in vain, as they say.

"I'm sure she does," he said smoothly. "Why a restaurant?"

"Because that's where chefs work?" I suggested, answering his question with one of my own. "People have to eat."

Did he think I had something to do with Erin's death? Or was he digging into something deeper?

"Some people operate food trucks," he said. "Those are mobile, easy to move from place to place. To—I don't know, disappear if you wanted to."

"You must know some interesting people who operate food trucks," I said. "I prefer to stay put and feed my regular customers. I'm not sure there's much call for the food I prepare at local fairs and carnivals anyway."

"You don't think people want lasagna?" he asked.

"Not as much as they want pizza and hamburgers," I said easily.

Personally, if I was going to go to a carnival, I'd love lasagna, but that was neither here nor there.

"You've been in New York for a long time, Chef St. James?"

"All my life," I said. "Apart from the occasional holiday. How about you?" I didn't really care, but if he was going to pretend to engage in small talk, two could play that game.

"Almost as long," he agreed. "Best place in the world."

"It definitely is. I see a table just opened up if

you'd like to have a seat." I had a feeling it wouldn't be that easy, not when he was sniffing around for something in particular.

Beside me, Cass moved with jerky movements like he was barely containing his irritation. I forced myself not to look at him and give him a reassuring glance. That wouldn't go unnoticed.

"What do you know about Toby Dent?" Getzoff, asked as if trying to catch me unaware.

I didn't need to pretend when I frowned. Was that his last name?

I shook my head. "Should I know who that is?"

"He's a convenience store owner who met with an unfortunate death a few nights ago," Getzoff said.

"I can't say it rings a bell," I said. "How terrible for him. And his family."

"Very terrible," Getzoff agreed. "The shelves in his storeroom weren't fastened to the wall correctly. They fell and he was crushed."

I winced. "That's awful. What a horrible way to die."

Getzoff was watching me carefully. Looking for my reaction. Possibly wondering if I'd give any sign I knew he wasn't killed by falling cans.

I cocked my head and frowned. "Wait a minute. Why do I get the feeling you're suggesting he didn't die that way?" I widened my eyes, leaned back and whispered, "Are you saying he was murdered? Do you think it's the same person that killed Erin?"

Was I convincing enough?

"Oh my god," Cass whispered. "What if there's a serial killer running around in the area?"

I looked over at him now and swallowed hard, trying not to lay it on too thick.

"Is that why you're here?" I asked, turning back to Getzoff. "Do you think I'm in some kind of danger?"

"I'm not sure." For the first time, he seemed to be on the back foot, as if he hadn't expected our reaction. "There does seem to be someone killing people. But the pattern is…"

He shook his head and pressed his lips together like he'd said too much already.

"Maybe I've watched too many episodes of *Criminal Minds*, but is it common for a serial killer to kill men and women?" I asked.

Personally, I never killed another woman until Gina. I knew Erin and Toby Dent had very different profiles: different ages, different personalities. She was innocent. He was not. On paper, they'd look unrelated. Wouldn't they?

"Not usually, but something tells me these two cases are related," he said. "Call it instinct if you like."

Something in his expression suggested I shouldn't call it instinct, but I wasn't sure what it was. Not unless he was involved with Hypnos and Zeus in some way.

There were too many witnesses for me to pull out a knife, end him and make him disappear. Not to mention I couldn't prove anything. He might be an innocent police officer doing his job. Nothing more.

Yeah, okay. And I was the second reincarnation of Darth Vader.

Still, just because he wasn't innocent didn't mean he was guilty. I saw that quote on a sign somewhere for a law firm. Archer would probably know the exact one, but I didn't, not off the top of my head.

"You think whoever killed her and him are the same person, and might eat here?" Cass asked.

I wanted to thank him for the question, if only to give me a few more moments to think.

"Have you noticed anyone suspicious who eats here regularly?" Getzoff asked.

"You've been in here a few times," I said with a laugh.

Also, the answer was yes. If you counted me, Cass, Boner, Archer, and Jules. Not to mention Gina.

When it came down to it, it was a good question whether he had anything to do with Hypnos and Zeus or not. If they knew who I was, they might well come in here and eat. Watch me. Make plans against me.

Finally, I shook my head. "No one comes to mind. I have a lot of regulars, but I can't say anyone looks more suspicious than anyone else."

"What about your staff?" Getzoff slid a glance toward Cass.

"I trust my staff implicitly," I said, trying to keep my annoyance in check at the not very subtle accusation. "Especially him. Does he look like he'd murder someone?"

I gestured toward Cass.

"Looks can be deceiving," Getzoff pointed out, giving me a direct look.

Okay, touché. I'd give him that point.

Cass held his hands up in front of himself.

"I've never killed anyone, I promise." That was true, he hadn't.

Yet.

He'd been a party to several deaths, but never wielded the knife. Or the acid. Or the water.

Getzoff pressed his lips together, frustrated. "If you think of anything, contact me. Something is going on here and I want to know what it is."

"Honestly, so do I," I told him. "If we're in any kind of danger, I'd like to know about it. Should I be watching my back?" With him or in general. Take your pick.

"It's always a good idea to watch your back, Chef

St. James," Getzoff said. He nodded, tucked his hands into his pockets, and strode back out the door.

"I trust him as far as I can throw him," Cass said softly.

"Me too," I agreed with a sigh. "I can't figure it out. Either he thinks we're into something, or he's trying to protect us, in a general 'cops trying to look after the public' kind of way."

"I don't think he knows which one it is," Cass said. "I know what instincts are like; they tell you something is up, but they don't tell you what."

"That's true," I said. "Mine are telling me not to trust him, but I want to think he doesn't mean us any harm."

"But you don't, do you?" he asked.

I rubbed my forehead with the heel of my hand. "I don't know what to think. He was definitely fishing for information. Trying to see if we knew anything about Toby Dent. Seeing if we'd make a mistake somehow."

"Do you think we did?"

"I don't think so," I said carefully. "I think we were vague and playing the victim or potential victim well enough to put him off our scent for now."

"Right." Cass toyed with the clip in his hair like he wanted to pull it out and let it fall over his eyes. He twisted his lips.

"I'm starting to think Jules is right. We should keep a low profile."

"That might be what they want," I said.

He blinked a couple of times before he grasped what I was getting at.

"You think there's a chance he was sent by them. To get you to back off?"

"If I was them, I'd try to scare us off," I said. "Then I'd wait, and make a move against us."

"When you asked if we should watch our back…"

"The answer is definitely yes," I said. "Watch it like we have a rearview mirror built into our heads."

He snorted softly. "That would be useful right now."

"It would. Come on, we have a few more desserts to make. Then we can get out of here for the night."

I hadn't forgotten about his implied suggestion back home, that he was going to fuck my mouth. I was more than ready for it after the conversation with the detective.

I wasn't going to stop living my life.

# CHAPTER 16

## HARLOW

As usual when someone has plans, the universe has other plans.

All of the night's customers decided to linger over their cups of coffee for a while, enjoying the conversation and each other's company.

Cass and I had the kitchen cleaned up. I sent Shelly and Yvette home for the night. We could handle cleaning up the last table once the customers finished up and left.

"Should I tell them to leave?" Cass said, looking like he might step over and order them out the door.

"No," I said with a sigh. "Let them enjoy the rest of the evening for a while longer. They'll leave when they're ready."

I'd give them another half an hour before I kicked them out. Part of being a good host meant not being pushy when people were relaxing, even if I had other plans.

"Can you tell them it's an emergency?" He adjusted the front of his pants.

I pressed my chest against his and gave him a kiss. "Is it?"

"Yes," he said, his voice strained. "Unless you want me to pop."

"Not after we just finished cleaning up," I said, with a small laugh.

He gave me a look like he was hoping for more sympathy than that. Truthfully, he might not be the only one who was going to pop. I'd ruined my panties a couple of hours ago.

"You know what Boner would say," he whispered.

"Lingering after dinner is not a good reason to… dispose of someone," I said firmly. "No matter how needy we are."

Cass sighed, but I saw the smile he was trying to hold back. The anticipation. He could wait a little longer, and had no intention of killing my customers. Unless, of course, they came at us first.

I quickly checked on them. Just in case.

They were pushing their chairs back, laughing over something before they headed out the door.

*"Thank fuck."* Cass said, drawing the words out. He trotted over to lock the door behind them. He

even had the presence of mind to pick up the last of the coffee cups and carry them into the kitchen. He had them in the dishwasher and the machine on before he turned to me.

"Now, where were we?"

I leaned back against the counter and regarded him.

"Unless I'm mistaken, we were discussing how frustrated we were."

"That's a good place to start." He stalked toward me, pressed his hands to the countertop on either side of me, boxing me in.

"I've been frustrated all night, waiting to get you alone."

"You have?" I cocked my head and gave him an innocent smile. "Why is that?"

"Because I can't resist you," he said, carefully enunciating each word at a time. "The first time I saw you, I couldn't even breathe."

"You could order a milkshake," I said teasingly, even though my heart was racing like crazy.

"You make the best milkshakes." He leaned in until his nose was brushing my cheek. "You make the best noises when you come. You make me crazy." He hesitated for a moment before adding, "Crazier than I already was."

He slammed his mouth down on mine, cutting

my laughter off. He slid his tongue against my lips, pressing them open and pushing inside. Slowly, he explored my mouth, tasting me and reminding me how he felt about me. As if I could possibly forget.

Working his hands under my chef jacket, he ran them up the back of my shirt and over my skin, unhooking my bra when he reached the strap. He pulled it down and cupped my breasts under my clothes.

"Everything about you is perfect," he said. He kneaded my breasts gently, making my nipples hard.

I shoved out of my jacket, pulled off my shirt and let my bra drop to his wrists. He pulled them away so it could fall to the floor, adding to the rapidly growing pile of clothes.

Tugging my hand, he drew me down to my knees, then onto my back on the floor. He got to work pulling off my shoes, socks and pants. Then grabbed my panties and pulled them away.

"If you could work like that…" he said admiring my bare body.

"I'd risk getting burned," I pointed out.

"We wouldn't want that." He lowered himself to his elbow beside me and tickled my stomach with the tip of his tongue, then gradually worked his way up, kissing my skin, my breasts, lavishing attention on one nipple, then the other.

His hand went the other way, moving down my stomach and between my thighs.

"You're so wet," he marveled. "So incredible."

"*You're* incredible," I told him, letting my legs fall apart wider so he could slide his hand up and down my pussy, and his fingers inside me.

"I'm incredibly lucky," he said. He fucked me harder with his hand, spreading my arousal around my pussy, making me slick. At the same time, he took off his own clothes, throwing things in all directions.

"On your hands and knees," he said, his dominant side reasserting itself again. He slid his hand out of me and slapped my ass as I scrambled to do what he told me.

He grabbed my thighs, pulling them apart before pressing his face between my legs, licking all around my pussy and up to my rear hole. I quivered with every sensation he sent all the way through my core.

"Cass," I whispered.

"Harlow," he whispered back, at the same volume and with the same urgency.

"Are you mocking me?" I asked, looking at him over my shoulder.

He grinned. "Never," and went back to lapping at me.

With a groan, he pulled his mouth back, knelt

behind me and pushed the tip of his cock into my pussy. Then the rest of him in one swift thrust.

"How do you do that?" he asked once he was fully seated inside me. "How do you feel even better every time?"

"I was going to ask you the same thing," I said. Each time he was inside me was better than the last.

He took his time fucking me. Pulling out slowly and sliding back in. Carefully and methodically. He pushed his hand between us and stroked my clit just as slowly. Inching us forward, one step at a time.

"Come for me," he insisted.

I could have argued with him, could have tried to hold on, but I'd been thinking about this for hours. One more touch on my clit and I was spiraling. Shattering into so many pieces, I wasn't sure they'd come back together in the same way when I came back down.

I caught my breath and took stock. All my parts seemed to be intact. My hair had come out of my bun and tumbled down around my face. Apart from that, I was whole.

Speaking of holes, Cass was still thrusting into mine, still slow and deliberate, until his body stilled, his hands jerked against my hips, and he came, coming inside me with a grunt that almost sounded frustrated, like he'd been trying to make himself last for longer but couldn't hold on anymore. He thrust into me a couple more times before sagging over me and sliding out.

"Magic," he whispered. "That's what you are."

I lowered myself onto my ass and smiled. "Of course I am. I'm really a witch. Didn't you notice the cauldron over in the corner?" I jerked my head toward the oven. "It's the modern version."

"That explains everything." He sat down beside me, his now flaccid, damp cock in his lap. "You put a love potion in the food."

"Only in your food," I told him. "And Boner and Archer."

"And Jules," he said.

"I don't know about that," I said.

"I do." He rubbed the ball of my foot. "You may not be able to see it. He might not even realize it yet. But he's head over heels. Almost as much as I am."

"Almost as much?" I asked.

He glanced up and grinned. "I know what I feel. I'm pretty sure no one comes close to it. They probably think they do, but they're wrong."

"You seem very sure of that," I teased lightly. Not casting aspersions on his feelings, but love was something we couldn't measure, especially in someone else.

"I'm more sure of that than I've ever been of

anything else," he said, leaning over to kiss my ankle. "Have you ever thought about getting a tattoo there?"

I glanced down. "I thought about it, but never got around to it. I guess I've been prioritizing these." I nodded toward the lines on my arm and the strikes through five of them. "Have you?"

"Not on my ankle," he said. "Maybe something on my shoulder. Do you think it would be too obvious if I got a picture of you and the words 'Chef Stabby?'"

I laughed. "It would raise a few questions. Especially if Detective Getzoff saw it."

We might as well wave a flag over our heads to say, 'Here we are. The people you're looking for. The people who know the answers to the questions you have.'

"Maybe something else then," he said.

I opened my mouth to say something, then closed it again.

"What is it?" He tilted his head and frowned at me. He seemed worried I was keeping a secret from him.

Tentatively, I said, "I was going to tease you but it might be in poor taste."

"Try me," he challenged.

If he insisted. "I was going to suggest you could get a picture of meatballs tattooed on you."

He stared at me for a moment, then laughed,

sticking his tongue out at the same time. "That's one for the maybe pile."

"I have a feeling the maybe pile is going straight into the dumpster out the back." I jerked my head in that direction.

"Well…" he drawled.

I laughed again. "I don't have an appropriate sense of humor. That's how I get by."

He exhaled softly out his nose, and switched to my other foot. "Me too. That and milkshakes. Jules uses anger to get out his frustration."

"I noticed that. Do you think it helps?" I leaned my back against the cabinet.

"Sometimes," he said. "Sometimes it makes things worse. He'll say things that'll upset other people. When they bite back, he gets angrier."

"Like me," I suggested.

"No," he said quickly. "You stick up for yourself. That's different. Everything you give him, he deserves. Same with Boner and Archer. But I think he likes arguing with all of you. And me."

"So you're saying arguing is his love language?" I asked.

"Something like that." He grimaced. "He's always been like that. Even as a kid he was the grumpy one. The one most likely to get the whole class kept in for detention. He was always getting into fights with other kids, usually verbal, sometimes physical, often when defending me and Auggie."

"I can't imagine you needed much defending," I said. He was nice, and laid back. More likely to go with the flow than someone like his brother or me. There was an intensity, but he kept it under wraps until the right time.

"I didn't, but Jules did it anyway," Cass said. "Sometimes I think he enjoys picking fights."

"I'm shocked," I said sarcastically. "Just shocked. Okay, not that shocked." I wasn't even surprised.

Cass chuckled. "I know, he doesn't hide it very well, does he?"

Once again I laughed.

"Not at all," I said. "But that's okay. It's part of what makes him him. It'd be boring if we were all the same."

"Unless we were all the same as Boner," Cass said. "Things would be…interesting."

"Interesting is one word for it," I agreed. We'd be laughing a lot, never taking anything seriously. Now I thought about it, that sounded pretty good.

Reluctantly, I said, "We should get home. The others will want to know Detective Getzoff was sniffing around again."

They weren't going to like it. I knew I didn't.

# CHAPTER 17

## ARCHER

was finding it more and more difficult to convince myself I shouldn't kill Detective Hans Getzoff.

Between the fact he was sniffing around Harlow, and that he apparently knew more than he was letting on, he was starting to become trouble.

In my experience, when you had trouble, you dealt with it. At least, as much as possible.

And if you couldn't deal with it, you avoided it.

Since he kept turning up like a fart after Taco Tuesday, avoiding him was apparently not going to happen.

Now I was hungry for tacos.

"He admitted they know Toby Dent was murdered?" I asked.

"He didn't come out and say as much," Harlow

said. "He let us come to that conclusion and he didn't disagree."

"Sounds like he was trying to profile you," I said, getting more aggravated.

"He doesn't know anything," she assured me. "He's looking for an angle. He could be stopping at every single business in the neighborhood, asking the same questions."

"You really think that?" I rubbed a hand over the stubble on my cheek.

"No," she said with a sigh. "I think he's looking for a connection between Toby Dent and Erin. I can't tell him who killed her since Gina was dead long before Toby."

"We could name someone we don't like," Boner suggested. "I don't mind throwing an arsehole under the bus to get the heat off us."

"Like who?" Harlow swiveled around in her chair and looked at him.

"Don't suggest me." Jules glowered, looking up from his phone before turning back to whatever he was doing. Not watching porn. It looked like something boring, like his bank app.

"What makes you think I was going to suggest you?" Boner asked.

"Because I've met you," Jules said, without

glancing in his direction. He tapped at something on the screen and his scowl deepened.

"And I've met you." Boner grinned. "How does it feel to be one of the chosen ones?"

Still without looking up, Jules flipped him off.

"He knows he's lucky." Boner chuckled. "He's keeping his cards close to his chest."

Jules smirked. "Come up with someone else. I'm sure there's plenty of people out there you don't like. On the other hand, it might be easier to find someone who doesn't like you."

Boner pressed a hand to his chest as though deeply offended. "There are people out there who don't like me?" he asked with mock disbelief. "Couldn't be."

Jules rolled his eyes and turned off his phone before placing it down on the coffee table in front of him. "We can't just give him a name. The moment he looks into it, he's going to see it's full of shit."

"Unless it's not," I said.

I tried not to shrink back when they all turned their attention to me. Sometimes being around so many people was a lot.

"We keep saying there's lots of assholes and predators out there," I said slowly.

"I think you just repeated yourself," Boner remarked.

I considered that for a moment.

"All predators are assholes, but not all assholes are predators."

He pointed a finger gun at me and clicked his tongue, conceding the point.

"Anyway, we find one and give his name to Getzoff," I said. "Someone plausible."

"Someone like you?" Jules suggested. He didn't sound malicious, just stating the fact that I more or less fit the description.

"Archer isn't an asshole," Cass said.

"I'm a predator." I uncrossed my knees and crossed them the other way, my arm on the couch behind Harlow. "I tracked down these people. That's what it makes me, isn't it?"

"In a way," Harlow agreed reluctantly. "But then so am I. And Getzoff already knows I exist. You too. Not," she added quickly, "that any of us is going to give your name to him."

She glanced around like she needed to be sure everyone was listening. Including Jules. Her gaze settled on him for longer than the rest of us.

"I could volunteer as bait, but I have a feeling that's a long game," Boner said. "Arrests. Court appearances. Prison. Becoming someone's bitch. All that shit."

"We're not using you as bait, either," Harlow said.

"We need to find someone who deserves it. Someone we'd take care of ourselves, under other circumstances."

"Right now we need to cover our asses, and keep Getzoff busy," Boner said.

"That too," Harlow agreed. "If we could find Hypnos and Zeus, that would be perfect. Getzoff could deal with them for us."

"Or they could deal with him," I said unapologetically.

"They could deal with each other," Cass suggested.

Boner snapped his fingers. "That's perfect. Can we do that?"

"Have you found them yet?" Jules asked him, his tone bone dry.

"It's on my to-do list," Boner said. "Right at the top, as a matter of fact. It's one of those tasks that doesn't seem to be crossed off when it should be." He pressed his lips into a line with annoyance.

Harlow rubbed the tattoos on her arm, the lines for the five men she'd crossed off her to-do list. I knew how frustrated she was that the other two remained elusive. I was frustrated too. They were out there. Until they weren't, she wouldn't get the peace she needed. She'd always be watching and waiting, either to find them or for them to come after us.

I'd spent too many sleepless nights searching for clues for those two. Either speaking to contacts or searching parts of the internet no sane person should venture into. Which, to be fair, was most of the internet, but some places are worse than others. How many predators had I found that way? And yet, not the two we really wanted.

They were good. Which probably meant they were powerful and virtually untouchable. The thing about the virtually untouchable, though, they posed a challenge none of us could resist. Not me anyway. I loved a good puzzle. And I loved to remind powerful people they were as mortal as I was. Acid was fun for that, a nice slow reckoning. Face to face with everything they'd done before their hearts came to a stop.

"What if we put out word that Getzoff was closing in on Hypnos and Zeus?" Cass suggested.

Now we were all staring at him.

"They'd go after him," Harlow said, as if she didn't quite believe what she was saying herself.

"What if this guy hasn't done anything wrong?" Jules suggested. "We could be dooming him when he's innocent."

"He's a detective; shouldn't he be able to handle anything?" Boner asked.

"He's a detective, not an immortal." Harlow said. "But that gives me an idea."

We all leaned in toward her while she spoke, nodding and offering suggestions.

"This could work," I said finally.

"If we do it right, it'll work," Boner said, with his usual confidence.

"If it doesn't, we're either dead or fucked," Jules said, as impressed as always. Which is to say he looked at us like he thought we were out of our minds. While at the same time accepting it might be the best idea any of us could come up with.

Either way, he wasn't offering anything better.

"Let's do it," Harlow said.

"We could kill three birds with one stone." Boner seemed pleased with that. "I always knew Harlow was the smartest one here."

"I don't know about that," Harlow said. "It's the logical thing to do, that's all."

"It's logical until it gets us dead," Jules said. He looked torn between agreeing to go along with the idea and getting up, walking out of my apartment and never looking back.

Evidently, Harlow and his brother overruled his sense of self-preservation because he stayed put for now.

"Then we don't let it get us dead." Cass gave him a look, like daring him to disagree. If there was something Jules knew how to do, it was disagree. He was as intimidated by the look as anyone would expect. He rolled his eyes and smirked.

"Manifesting is only going to get us so far, little brother," he said. "We need a lot of planning and a whole shit ton of luck."

"Then we plan," Harlow said. "We plan and pull this thing off."

————

Boner

I have to say Harlow was hot when she was making plans to take over the world. Okay, okay. Take down her enemies. Either way.

She was making my cock harder and harder the more I sat and listened to her. The minute this conversation was over, I was going to drag her off and fuck her brains out. Or maybe I'd stay here with the rest of them and we could all fuck her brains out together. Yeah, that sounds like the perfect plan.

————

Archer

•  •  •

This is my book, bro.

————

Boner

Yeah, you don't mind me helping you out a little bit here and there, right? I mean, everyone wants to know what's going on in my head. Right?

————

Archer

I don't.

I turned back to the conversation. Harlow had found one of my notepads on my desk and started to write down our plan, outlining everything everyone needed to do and where we all needed to be.

Boner was right about one thing. She was hot as hell when she was doing this. I gave him a look to remind him not to interrupt again. He'd had his say. He didn't need to jump on mine.

Okay, I didn't mind too much. As long as he

didn't intrude when I was fucking our woman. That would be annoying.

Boner opened his mouth to say something, but closed it again, giving me a smile before he turned to speak to Harlow instead.

"Should I hold another party at the gallery? We know Getzoff likes those."

"And the bad guys," Harlow said.

Her eyes glazed, remembering how Solomon Danforth was at that party. They'd spoken briefly. He was an old friend of her father, a former mentor. She had no way of knowing he was really Eros, not until he revealed himself.

His identity, that is, not his dick. I'd say lucky for him, but he ended up dead anyway. And in several pieces. His death was one of the most satisfying, I have to say. Because of what he was to Harlow and because I might have held a grudge after he tied me to a chair. If there was anything I hated, it was being confined like that. Also thinking I might die at any moment. That wasn't fun either.

"Another party would be too obvious," I said. "What about something at one of the restaurants?"

"We've already had the grand opening," Harlow said regretfully. She seemed frustrated, like we squandered the perfect opportunity to trap our enemies "There's nothing else on the itinerary. The place is booked out for the next year at least." She should be celebrating that, not looking like someone kicked her kitten.

"What about Angel's Rest?" Cass asked. "I know it's smaller but maybe something there." He toyed with the hair that hung over his forehead, like he couldn't decide if he should shove it back out of the way or pull it down further. Torn between hiding himself and leaving himself exposed.

"That's a good idea," I said slowly.

I told Harlow what to add to the list, and she wrote them down in her neat, precise handwriting. Of course she even wrote prettily.

Finally, she tossed the notepad and pen onto the table in front of her and leaned back. "Until then, we might as well get some rest."

"I have an idea before we get any rest," I said, reaching for her.

# CHAPTER 18
## HARLOW

For the second time in a handful of hours, I found myself naked, this time stretched out on the couch, not on the kitchen floor, and surrounded by four men, not one. In spite of having fucked Cass earlier, I was ready for another round, almost as though I hadn't had an orgasm at all.

Cass said something to Boner, who nodded and knelt down beside him, in front of me.

Together they eased my legs apart and inched forward between them, the sides of their faces pressed against the insides of my thighs.

Boner's tongue flicked out, teasing my pussy, making me quiver.

Then it was Cass' tongue, as he did the same thing.

Without any particular rhythm, they took turns,

tasting me and teasing me, lapping at my clit. Every so often they'd break away from me and kiss each other in a mashing of lips and tongues and arousal.

They broke away from each other and exchanged a glance and a nod.

Boner eased a finger inside me, his hand palm up. Cass did the same but palm down, below Boner's, so their knuckles were rubbing against each other, fingers stroking my insides.

My eyes widened.

"Oh my god," I whispered. One of them fucking me with their hand was amazing. Two of them was out of this world. Could this get any better?

As if he read my mind, Archer inched over and knelt beside me, stroking his engorged cock with his hand.

One hand on the couch for balance, I wrapped the other around his length, stroking him right in front of my face. So close I could smell the pre-cum on his tip.

I turned my face and licked, wanting, needing, to taste him.

He groaned. "You have the best tongue," he whispered.

"You taste delicious," I told him.

The couch moved as Jules knelt on the other side.

"How do I taste?"

I turned my face and almost bumped my nose

into his cock. At the last moment, I lifted my chin so my mouth found him instead. I ran my tongue over his slit and tasted him.

"You taste different from Archer, but just as delicious," I told him.

If I closed my eyes and tasted one and then the other, I could tell them apart, even after that small sample. Jules' arousal tasted saltier, and Archer had a hint of sweetness that was unexpected.

Together, they were a complex dish with layered flavors that left a whole new experience in the back of your mouth after you swallowed.

I drew Jules' cock into my mouth and sucked until my cheeks hollowed out. Then popped off him and turned back to Archer, giving him the same lavish treatment.

Boner and Cass were taking turns stroking my G-spot while the other toyed with my rear hole. Pressing their finger inside lightly and rubbing it around.

I had to keep switching between Archer and Jules to keep myself from coming too soon. It was difficult with two very different fingers inside me, not to mention the sight of both men with their eyes on my pussy and then on each other, exchanging kisses here and there and groaning into each other's mouths.

Eventually, Jules had enough of sharing. He

tangled my hair around his fist and frantically fucked my mouth, making me gag, but never stopping.

If anything, every time I gagged, he drove in faster, harder and deeper.

"Look at you, you fucking whore," he whispered. "You have four men here, touching you and fucking you, and you love every minute of it."

I groaned my agreement and gripped his balls in my hand, holding them hard, massaging them, working him until he exploded in the back of my throat so hard I thought I'd choke.

He barely caught his breath before he was yanking himself out of me and shoving my face onto Archer's cock. Hand still in my hair he worked me hard and fast, while Archer hung on, trying to keep up with him.

"Don't hold back," Jules told him. "She needs this. She wants us to use her body. She loves it because we own her. Don't we?"

He tightened his grip on my hair until I thought he might tear out a clump.

I made no attempt to pull away. Jules was right, I was enjoying this, giving and receiving pleasure, even as rough as this. I wanted more.

Archer thrust a little faster, a little harder. More tentative than Jules had been, but still vigorous.

Right before Archer came, I did. Screaming out

around his cock and gasping for air. Almost choking again when he shattered, spilling himself into my mouth.

He barely had time to pull out of me before Cass was picking me up off the couch.

"Lie back." He waited for Boner to do what he said before he pressed me into a straddle over Boner's hips.

"Lean forward," Cass snapped.

Still trying to catch my breath, I did as he said, resting my head on Boner's chest and listening to his heart thump.

Hands on my stomach, Cass lifted me up. He positioned my pussy over Boner's cock and lowered me down onto it.

I heard the click of a tube and cool fingers smeared lube on my rear hole. Then Cass knelt behind me and eased a finger inside my ass, smearing the lube around, stretching me out with one finger, then a second.

"Please," I whispered. He added a third finger, filling me up until I was almost ready to scream.

I needed more. I almost cried when he pulled his fingers out, but then he was replacing them with his cock, easing inside inch by inch, stopping to give me time to get used to him before pushing on.

"Holy shit," Boner whispered when Cass was fully seated inside me. "Hello there, Cass' cock."

Cass snorted softly. "Hello yourself."

"Hello both of you," I said with a laugh. I'd never felt so full in my life, with a man in each of those holes. So deep and thick.

Carefully, slowly, they started to move. Sliding in and out of me in unison, almost like they'd done this a hundred times before.

Boner held me gently, his hands on my hips, helping me to rise and fall, to create friction with him without dislodging Cass.

It took a few moments to get it right but soon we were all moving in unison. Breathing in unison too, I noticed. Ragged breaths. Slick with sweat.

I closed my eyes and focused on rolling my hips the right way. Enjoying the sensations, the smells, the sounds. Both of them were grunting and groaning as they thrust. Those were not in unison, so I could enjoy them both. The whole thing together was like a beautiful symphony. All the right ingredients placed together just so, for the perfect balance.

If I could make this into a meal, I'd make a fortune. Not that I'd share it with the world. No, this was just for us. For me and my men.

For once, no one was barking orders. I don't think

Cass could have managed coherent words if he wanted to. I certainly couldn't.

Archer and Jules sat in separate armchairs, both watching us avidly. Jules' expression suggesting I was the dirty whore he called me, but not in a bad way. He was appreciating that I enjoyed sex, loving the show we were putting on for him, committing it to memory for later.

"I've died," Boner said. Apparently he was the only one here capable of putting thought into words. "I've died and gone to heaven. This is why you call your restaurants 'Angels'? Right, love? Because you are one."

I managed to smile. I was no angel. Right now I only wanted to be me. Right here in this moment.

Whatever happened after this, we'd have tonight.

I chastised myself for thinking that. We'd have more than that. We had to. I needed to do this a lot more. I liked to practice something until I got it right. This would definitely take approximately…oh, fifty years of practice, maybe more. It was a study I could devote myself to without any qualms.

I might even sell my restaurants and spend the rest of my life being double stuffed. I read about it in books, but the reality was almost indescribable. Full, hot, sticky perfection. Like pizza, but better.

Without warning, another orgasm washed over

me. Even stickier and more perfect. More intense than the ones which came before. No pun intended.

This one was trying to swallow me whole while shattering me at the same time. Breaking me like I'd never been broken before, only to put me back together.

I cried out. Rolled my hips harder, chasing the bliss. Wanting to make it last for longer. Forever, if possible. That didn't seem like too much to ask.

Boner was a moment behind me, thrusting up into me. Muttering a string of words that I couldn't make out. Something along the lines of, "Oh fucking good gravy fucking yeah fuck amazing yes."

Approximately.

I could have the order of that wrong.

A moment after him was Cass' turn. His fingers dug into my hips as his body stilled. I felt the rush of heat into my ass as he flooded me with his cum.

Hands trembling, Cass slowly slid out of me and flopped down on the edge of the couch. So close, he almost fell off.

Boner chuckled.

"So graceful, little bro," Jules called out.

Cass' face was buried in the side of the couch beside my bicep. He said something muffled that sounded like, "I'd flip you off but I can't be bothered."

Jules barked a laugh. "Don't act like you didn't like it."

None of us was going to do that. We'd all had a thoroughly good time with each other. Not one regret from any of us.

Except…this had to end for now. That was inevitable, I supposed. We all had to sleep at some point. The curse of being mere humans.

"Hey Cass," Boner said, "I don't care what other ideas you've had in your entire life. That was the best one. Ever."

Cass lifted his face and looked over at us, his eyes all but obscured by his hair.

"Yeah it was." He flopped his face back down.

I smiled. "I agree with Boner. That was a very good idea," I said.

"I have another slightly less good idea," Boner said. "Let's get you into the bath and clean you up." He eased me off his cock, letting his cum trickle back out of me and mingle with Cass'.

"Also a good idea." I let them help me off the couch before Boner swept me up in his arms and carried me to the bathroom. I kicked my legs in some kind of protest, but he held me tighter, pulling me against his firm body.

"I'll get the water." Archer trotted past us, his cock slapping against his thighs as he went.

"I'll make some coffee or some shit," Jules said.

"I'll help you," Cass said, following me and Boner into the bathroom.

He opened the cabinet and started to pull out bath salts and shampoo, along with a clean, fluffy towel.

"I'm going to be spoiled, aren't I?" I asked, lying in Boner's arms while Archer filled the bath.

"If we have anything to say about it, yes you are," Boner agreed. "Very, very spoiled."

I had a feeling even if I tried to argue, they wouldn't listen. They were going to pamper me if it was the last thing they did.

I hoped like hell it wasn't.

# CHAPTER 19

## HARLOW

"Thank you for joining us this evening."

Detective Getzoff stepped into Angel's Rest in a store bought suit, his hair slicked back.

"I was surprised to be invited," he said. "You seem…uncomfortable in my presence."

"I don't trust people easily." I said honestly, "But you've shown your support for me and my restaurants. I thought I'd return the favor." I hoped it wasn't obvious I was lying through my teeth.

Again.

"Feel free to mingle with the other guests. Dinner will be along shortly."

"Thank you, Chef St. James." He stepped farther inside, nodding to someone.

I turned my face but couldn't figure out exactly who he was acknowledging.

Several of my regulars stood in roughly the right direction, including Judge Forest Cross and film critic Kevin Lotz-Moore.

I invited my most esteemed regulars. I owed them for continuing to come here and eat my food, especially after Erin was murdered here. A few notable others had stayed away. I didn't blame them; violent death would freak most people out.

Honestly, I'd thought about not coming back here myself, but this was my happy place. I put that night behind me as best I could and got on with it.

When it came down to it, they were the ones missing out on fine food. Although a couple of them were now eating at Angel's Redemption instead, so it worked out for everyone.

Except Erin.

I greeted the next handful of guests, giving them the same spiel, and laughing at their responses although I only half-heard.

No doubt they'd put it down to nerves. We didn't often hold events like this here. This was a small, intimate restaurant. Nothing fancy except for the food.

A special dinner like this was unique. If I had my way, I'd never do it again. All these people in this space made my anxiety levels spike.

I startled as someone put a hand on my shoulder. I spun around to see Boner, a drink in his hand.

"Sorry, love. Didn't mean to scare the shit out of you." He stroked his fingers over my neck.

"It's okay," I said quickly. "This is a lot."

"It is a lot. I'm impressed. I was just in the kitchen checking out the food. It looks tasty." He smacked his lips and leaned in to whisper, "Not as tasty as you."

"You didn't eat any of it, did you?" I eyed him as if the accusation was serious. The hint of a smile on my lips might have proven otherwise.

"A little nibble here or there, that's all." He gave me a wink. "You know me. I wouldn't ruin this for you."

"Of course you wouldn't," I said. "I should get back in there and make sure everything is ready. Shelly and Yvette can greet the rest."

They both looked at me like I needed a reminder they'd stood back while I did their job for them. Both were perfectly capable of doing it.

Yeah, I knew all of that, but I'd wanted to greet Getzoff personally, so he felt comfortable and relaxed tonight. He might need it.

"I'll come with you," Boner said. "Check that. There's someone over there I need to catch up with."

"Okay," I said as he kissed my cheek and hurried away.

I shrugged and worked my way through the customers who stood chatting to each other, and slipped back into the kitchen.

"How is everything?" I asked.

Cass was keeping an eye on the marinara sauce, his phone in his hand.

"Everything is in place," he said. "I've put out word that Detective Getzoff is looking into the deaths of Granger Fairfield and Solomon Danforth. Apparently he found a promising lead, connecting them to other people of influence."

I straightened my chef jacket and tried not to wince. It was one thing to use ourselves as bait, but to use someone else…

"We're all right here if anything happens," Archer said. He stood near the storeroom, soda in one hand, phone in the other, hiding from the crowds.

"I know," I said. "I wonder if we should warn him, that's all."

"If he's working with them, he might warn them," Archer said reasonably. "We don't need him to do that."

"This was your plan," Cass pointed out, as if I needed a reminder.

I straightened my ponytail and moved over to stir the sauce.

"I know. I also know it could go horribly wrong for everyone."

"It's going to go horribly *right*," he assured me. He stepped over behind me and bracketed my hips with his hands, leaning in to press a kiss to my neck. Drawing a shiver from me. "We've got this."

"Unless you're having second thoughts?" Archer asked.

"What are the statistics on people having second thoughts in situations like this?" I asked with a sigh.

"I don't know, but I'm going to guess it's high." He glanced at his screen like he might look for the answer there, but shook his head to himself.

"What's the percentage of people who get into situations like this?" I asked.

He took a moment to think about that. "I'm going to suggest it's low."

"Let me guess. Five people out of the millions that live in the city," I said.

"I might narrow it down to five out of the billions of people who live on the planet," he said. "Although, there might be more of us than we know."

"Oh, I don't know. Five sounds about right," I said laughing bitterly. "Everyone else is too sane for this bullshit."

"Are you calling us insane?" Cass asked, his breath brushing my earlobe.

"Unless you have a better word for it," I asked. "Unhinged. Out of our trees. Fucked up as fuck. Screwy." I exhaled out my nose.

"If this is unhinged, then I don't want to be hinged," Cass said, squeezing my hips.

"If Jules was here, he'd have something to say about that," I said.

Jules was outside, on the street, keeping an eye on comings and goings from the restaurant. A job he volunteered for. Possibly because he didn't trust the rest of us to be up to it. And possibly because he wanted some time alone, away from the craziness.

Right, there was another word, crazy.

What can I say, I wasn't a walking thesaurus.

"Yeah, he would," Cass agreed. "But he's as unhinged as the rest of us, so that doesn't count. Anyway, I don't give a shit if he approves or not. This is my life now. *You're* my life now." He kissed my cheek. His lips soft and reassuring.

"We should start plating up the first course," I said reluctantly.

Not reluctant to feed people, reluctant to step away from his embrace. It was comforting here. Warm and safe. Like the minute I stepped away, I was vulnerable again. I hated being vulnerable more than I hated almost anything.

Cass slipped his hands from me and stepped back

to grab plates and start putting them out so I could plate up the fig and prosciutto salad and freshly baked bread, which he'd been slicing while I was greeting guests. His knife work was getting better. The slices were almost perfectly uniform.

Even though I was a bundle of nerves, I noticed details like that. It was ingrained in me, for one thing. For another, obsessing took my mind off everything else.

"That looks so pretty," Archer said as I finished the first of the plates and made sure they were clean and ready to go.

"Thank you," I told him, turning my face far enough to kiss his cheek. His stubble was rough against my lips, but his body close to mine was as warm and comforting as Cass'.

Where once I would have preferred to do this alone, now I was glad for their presence.

Honestly, I wasn't sure if I could do this without them. I didn't want to. They were mine and I was theirs, no matter what happened.

I glanced out to the seating area and nodded to Yvette for her and Shelly to start herding the customers toward their tables.

With one eye on the rest of the plates, I watched Detective Getzoff move around the room before sitting at a table with Judge Cross and Kevin Lotz-Moore.

Interesting that was the company he chose to sit with. Both glanced at him speculatively, but returned to the conversation they were having between themselves. Nothing heavy by the look of it. One or the other would laugh every couple of minutes.

Getzoff said something to the man sitting beside him. A tall man with silver as his temples, who wore a leather jacket that looked expensive. His dark eyes regarded the detective with curiosity, but didn't seem to be unfriendly. He must have arrived with someone else. I couldn't remember seeing him here before.

They started off a conversation about who knows what. They were too far for me to hear. They could be talking about the weather for all I knew. Or how to eviscerate a corpse without making too much of a mess.

That sounded more like the conversations my men and I had around the dinner table, but who knew? Getzoff might secretly be a serial killer too.

I couldn't rule him out as the person who killed Lionel Gammage. For one thing, he arrived with the other cops remarkably fast after the man's death.

I shook my head to myself and finished plating up. Once the guests were seated, Shelly and Yvette hurried over to take out their salads and bread, plus a couple of plates for people with dairy intolerance who weren't able to eat the dressing on the salad. Plus a couple without prosciutto for my kosher guests.

The chatter died down for a while as everyone started to eat, replaced with smiles and groans of appreciation. The wine flowed freely. Shelly and Yvette moving around to fill up glasses as guests asked for more.

"Everyone seems to be having a nice time," Archer said.

"Mmmhmm," I agreed. Especially Boner. He was seated at a table with some other guests, positioned so he could keep an eye on everyone in the room. He was doing a good job of looking like he wasn't looking, while talking to the woman beside him, then telling a joke that made the whole table crack up laughing.

"You could sit out there too," I told him.

He shuddered. "I'm good here, thanks. It's easier to keep an eye on everyone."

It probably wasn't, but I wasn't going to call him out on it. If he didn't want to be there in the crowds, I wouldn't pressure him.

The atmosphere out there was relaxed, but with a hint of tension that was probably just me. It was palpable, pulled tighter than a guitar string.

Forcing a few deep breaths in and out, I started to make the pasta. Naturally everything was fresh. That's what my guests were paying for; a special evening of good food and good company. With the proceeds going to a shelter down the street from us.

They could eat well and be seen helping out other people, how better to soothe people's egos, while making Getzoff vulnerable?

If Cass sent the right message, Hypnos and Zeus would know exactly where he was tonight, and roughly what time he'd be walking down the street, possibly alone. It was one time where his whereabouts could be pinpointed.

Whether or not they'd act on it remained to be seen.

# CHAPTER 20
## HARLOW

My nerves were on edge all the way through the dinner service and into dessert. They didn't let up when guests started to rise and make their way out the door onto the street, most talking and laughing, full of wine and good company.

Judge Cross and Kevin Lotz-Moore were amongst the last to leave. Getzoff, and the men beside him, remaining at one table. Boner and a couple of people at another.

"I can't tell if this is anticlimactic or if things are about to get real," Cass said. He twisted his lips and thought about it but shook his head, coming to no conclusions one way or the other. He'd spent the whole evening in the kitchen, out of sight. His attention on work, and his phone for any updates to the information he'd put out there. If our enemies saw it, there was no indication.

Yet.

"I don't know either," I admitted. I leaned against him for a moment, my head on his shoulder, before I reluctantly stepped away. "I'm going to see if anyone wants coffee."

Making sure my jacket was straight, I stepped out into the sitting area and forced a smile as I headed over to Getzoff's table.

"Detective, I hope you had a nice time tonight," I said.

He looked up at me and smiled. "Thank you. I can't tell you how much I've enjoyed myself. It's been a while since I've eaten so well and in such good company." He nodded to the man beside him.

"That's good," I said, trying to sound sincere. "I was wondering if you'd like a cup of coffee.

"I'd love one," he said. "On one condition."

If I wasn't already on edge, that would have put me right there.

"What's that?" I asked carefully.

"You've been working hard all night," he said. "Sit down and join us."

"Don't mind if I do." Boner plopped down into a

chair opposite him, grinning at all of us. "Edward Bonegard." He offered his hand to Getzoff.

Getzoff shook it politely and looked back at me. Apparently he was serious with his request.

"I could sit down for a while," I said, grateful Boner would be there too. His table mates had already left, so him joining us now didn't look too suspicious.

I hoped.

"Excellent," Getzoff said.

"Yeah." I backed away and returned to the kitchen, where Cass already started the coffee machine.

"It might be safe for you to sit out with us now," I said to Archer, who was peering around the doorframe at Getzoff.

Very unsubtle, if I'm honest.

"Yeah, now most of the people have gone," he agreed. He slipped his phone into his pocket; the battery must have been almost dead by now. It hadn't left his hand all night.

He took a couple of cups of coffee Cass handed him and carried them out, placing one in front of Boner before sitting with him.

Between Cass and I, we took out the rest of the cups.

The man who'd sat beside Getzoff slipped out

while I spoke to Archer, leaving an eclectic group alone in the restaurant.

"Isn't this interesting?" Getzoff adjusted his tie and sat back in his chair.

"Is it?" Boner asked. "That's great. I love when things are interesting." He propped his elbow on the chair beside him and leaned over like he didn't have a care in the world. "Harlow tells us you think there's a serial killer in the area."

Thank goodness I hadn't taken a sip of coffee. I would have spat it out across the table. As it was, I coughed, choking on air.

"Did I say that?" Getzoff asked, looking around the table like we were all as suspicious as fuck. Which was accurate, but I didn't *think* he knew that. Not yet.

"You didn't deny it," I said. "Boner owns a gallery nearby. He has a vested interest in the safety of his clients."

"And my own ass," Boner said. "Which I am quite attached to, thank you very much. Meanwhile, isn't it the job of the police to warn us of shit like that?"

"It can be," Getzoff said carefully. "Sometimes the circumstances aren't that simple. For example, if we were to let everyone know what we were looking for, the perpetrator might go underground."

"Literal underground or figuratively?" Boner leaned forward to ask.

"Both," Getzoff said.

"Huh. That sounds like fun." Boner grinned. "I've been down in the subway tunnels a time or two myself. Can't say I've seen any serial killers in there, though." He scratched his head as though thinking about it.

"How would you know if you saw a serial killer?" Cass asked him.

"Well, they all look the part, don't they?" Boner asked, clearly having way too much fun with this. "Don't they look like Hannibal Lecter, and drink Chianti?"

I suppressed a grimace. I didn't drink Chianti or eat fava beans. Nor did I look like Anthony Hopkins. Or Ted Bundy for that matter.

Although I wouldn't lump myself in with Hannibal Lecter or Bundy. One was fictional and the other killed for the fun of it. Not with purpose. There was nothing noble about what he did. Nothing redeemable.

"On the contrary," Getzoff said. "Serial killers look like average people. They could look like anyone at this table."

"Including you," Boner suggested, turning the veiled accusation back on Getzoff.

"Including me," Getzoff agreed. "But I'm not a serial killer. I'm someone who catches them."

"*Oh?*" Boner asked, dragging the word out. "How many have you caught?"

Getzoff glared at him, like he was annoyed at being called out.

"I've uncovered the identities of multiple criminals," Getzoff said. "I'm going to find out who's behind the killings in the area."

"So you admit there's a serial killer in the area," Boner said. "What are we looking for here? Someone who offers candy for their victims to get into the back of a car? Wait, no, let me guess. Someone who dresses as Santa and lures people with the promise of presents. I might even be fooled by that one. I mean, who's going to think he's a bad guy?"

"Santa is creepy," Archer said. "When I was a kid, I refused to sit on his lap."

Boner pointed at him. "Those are good instincts, Harden. That wasn't actually Santa, it was a dude in a Santa suit. Possibly a woman. Maybe a non-binary Santa." He seemed to like that idea.

"Anyone who works with children is carefully vetted," Getzoff said, his voice tight with barely restrained agitation.

"Yeah, yeah." Boner flapped his hand like that was a minor detail.

"Hard*wick*," Archer interjected belatedly.

"So what are we looking for?" Boner asked. "I'd really like to avoid them if possible. How will we know what to avoid if we don't know anything about this person?"

"I'm not at liberty to discuss details of the case," Getzoff said. "My advice: be careful and don't walk around outside alone."

"Excellent advice." Boner clapped his hands. "I'll make sure to have a buddy with me everywhere I go."

A flash of irritation crossed his features. Getzoff leaned forward, placing his weight on his arms. "You don't seem to be taking this seriously, Mr. Bonegard."

"Call me Boner," Boner said. Which really did nothing to counter Getzoff's accusation. "I'm taking it very seriously, believe me. This is who I am. Take me or leave me." He spread his hand either side.

Getzoff looked like he'd take the 'leave me' option if he had a choice.

"Is there anything we can do?" I asked, trying to divert the conversation. "The killer could be someone we know. What do we do if they are?"

I hoped he was buying the potential damsel in distress routine. If I found another serial killer, I knew exactly what to do.

"You contact me immediately," Getzoff said. "Don't try to point fingers at them."

"We'd never do that, would we, Cass?" Boner said, pointing a finger at Cass.

Cass gave him a funny look and batted it away.

"What would we be looking for?" I asked, genuinely curious. It wouldn't hurt if I picked up a few tips to help me avoid being caught.

"Usually serial killers are loners," Getzoff said. "They either don't like the company of people, or people are uncomfortable around them."

"Luckily none of us fits into that description," I said, ignoring the fact Archer hid in the kitchen all evening. "In theory, we'd be looking at someone who comes in and eats alone?"

Getzoff was starting to fit into this description better than we were. Was he trying to draw attention away from himself? He was a police detective, but that didn't mean he was a good person.

"Potentially," Getzoff agreed, clearly seeing the comparison I'd raised. "They'd be unlikely to hold a conversation for very long. Nor would they enjoy a meal like tonight's."

"No offense, but you're starting to make serial killers sound really boring," Boner complained. "Makes you wonder why people watch all those serial killer documentaries."

"Those are interesting," Archer said. "Human psychology is fascinating. You'd be surprised what motivates people to do things."

"I don't know if I'd be *that* surprised," Boner said. "I've met some strange people in my life." He looked around the table and grinned.

Cass elbowed him in the bicep. "We're not strange," he said.

"That, dear Titmus the Younger, is a matter of opinion," Boner told him. "Don't worry though, being strange isn't a bad thing. Look at me, I'm strange."

"You don't say," I teased.

He blew me a kiss not offended in the slightest.

Did he have to be so adorable? Yes, I supposed he did. Otherwise, he wouldn't be Boner.

I covered a yawn with my fist. I'd been so wired all day, it was starting to catch up with me. I looked into my coffee only to see it was empty, a thin layer of the milky beverage in the corners of the cup. I should finish cleaning up.

I yawned again, blinking a couple of times. My eyelids were getting heavy.

"Yes, I should call it a night," Getzoff said, downing the last of his drink and placing his mug in front of him on the table.

He pushed his chair back and rose, blinked a couple of times and staggered. He tried to grab onto the edge of the table, but collapsed onto the floor with a thump, landing in front of the legs of his chair.

I blinked a couple of times myself, trying to get my head around what happened. I said something but it came out slurred. Why was I so tired?

I tried to stand, but my legs wouldn't hold me. I flopped back down, hard enough to hurt my ass. My vision was blurry. Was everyone else struggling to stand too, or was I seeing things?

Cass let out a groan, reached for me and missed. He fell against me, his weight bearing down. The feet scraped on the floor as we both fell off the chair and onto the floor in a heap.

We landed with his weight on top of me. Heavy, and horribly still.

I registered a jolt of pain in my arm before everything went black.

———

Archer

*Not again.*

That was my first thought as I slowly regained consciousness.

Whatever I was lying on, it was hard. Uncomfortable. It smelled clean, but with a lingering tinge of blood. That could just be me. The memory of it clung to my nostrils. It had since my first kill.

I forced my eyes to open, half-expecting a glare.

Instead, the light was dim. All I could see were the legs of tables and chairs. I was still in Harlow's restaurant. Lying on the floor, tied up like a pig.

Had Getzoff done this to us? If he had…

No, I remembered him falling. Hitting the floor. Whatever happened, he was a victim here too.

Lucky for him, he might avoid being a victim of me. Once I got out of this, that was.

Groaning, I managed to roll over, flopping onto my other side like a fish. Cass lay right in front of me. Boner too. They seemed to be breathing.

"What the hell?" That was Jules' voice.

The door closed behind him. His footsteps got closer. Then he was looming over all of us. Staring.

"What happened here?"

I'd like to know the answer to that myself. I parted my lips, but no words came. Thought was barely coherent, much less speech.

Cass groaned. Followed a few moments later by Boner.

Neither sound was loud, but they made my head pound. I felt as though I'd drunk an entire bottle of vodka and this was the morning after.

I hadn't had any alcohol. That might change when my hands were free. I could do with a drink right now. Maybe a few.

"Fuck." Jules hurried away. When he returned, he held a knife in his hand. He cut the zip ties off his brother first, then me, leaving Boner for last.

I sat up and rubbed my face. "Where's Harlow?"

# CHAPTER 21
## HARLOW

My head ached like a bitch. It pounded in time with my heartbeat.

I still had a heart to beat; that was a good thing, right? Okay, that depended on what happened in the next hour.

Right now, my hands and feet were tied almost tight enough to cut off the circulation. Was there any chance my men did this? They might have thought I'd enjoy being bound and fucked boneless.

I would. But I knew for certain that wasn't what was going on here.

I tried to blink. I could move my eyelashes slightly, nothing more.

No response came.

No Boner saying, "She's awake, fellows, let's go."

I'd never heard him say the word 'fellows,' but it fit with the scenario I was hoping for.

Pushing away the anxiety that stirred in my chest, tightening around my heart before traveling up to my neck and my already aching forehead.

*Think calm thoughts. You're alive. That's a start. Whatever's going on here, if they wanted you dead, you'd be dead.*

My throat was so dry, when I tried to swallow, it felt like my larynx was scraping against itself.

The inside of my mouth tasted bitter. What was the last thing I ate?

I remembered drinking coffee in my restaurant. This wasn't the bitter aftertaste from the delicious beverage. No, this was something else. Did someone slip something into my drink?

Cass fell against me.

Getzoff. He was there too, wasn't he? Yes, he fell before the rest of us. It wasn't my drink that was spiked, it was all of ours.

Someone was in a whole heap of shit when I got out of here. I didn't call myself Chef Stabby for nothing. This was going to come out in all its bloody glory. Whoever did this to us, I was going to *fuck them up.*

I swallowed again and tried to open my eyes. Why did I have sandpaper in my tear ducts?

I blinked it away and glanced around.

Wherever I was, it was dark. The floor underneath was concrete, cold and hard. Perfect for breaking heads.

Other people's heads, not mine.

"Miss St. James," a voice said. Smooth as silk.

I responded with an angry hum, and tried to sit up. The pounding in my head worsened.

"How nice of you to join us." he said.

Definitely a male voice. Not Getzoff. Not any of my men either.

I tried to place it, but I didn't recognize whoever they were.

"What do you want?" I managed to croak out.

"I was wondering the same thing," he said.

Before I could ask, a groan sounded from beside me. What was Detective Getzoff doing here?

I turned my face far enough to see him a couple of feet away. His wrists and ankles were bound as well.

"I heard a rumor." A chair creaked as our captor rose. His silhouette was slender as he moved around the room. "The rumor is, the good detective here might be investigating me and my associates."

Understanding came crashing in on me.

There was a reason they called him Hypnos. It wasn't because he hypnotized people. He drugged them to get them under his control. Men like him, they thrived on power.

I had to keep that thought in my mind. Try not to give him power over me. At the same time, try not to threaten him too much. If his back was against the wall, he'd come out swinging.

Right now he held all the cards.

"What are you talking about?" Getzoff asked. He struggled to sit up and stare into the shadows. "I'm hunting a serial killer."

Of course he was forthcoming with that information now. He wanted to save his own skin, didn't he? Fair enough. That was why I was here too, in a manner of speaking.

I glanced around.

None of my men were here as far as I could see. What had he done with them? Were they…

No way I was going to finish *that* thought. That would lead to despair. If I despaired, I wouldn't try as hard to get the hell out of here.

No, they were out there looking for me. They had to be.

"Perhaps Miss St. James can cast some light on the issue," our captor said. "The information came from her restaurant."

I screwed my eyes shut. Cass would have done all

he could to cover his tracks. Evidently it wasn't enough.

"You see," Hypnos went on, "we've been keeping an eye on you and your establishment."

"Oh yeah?" I asked. My voice sounded stronger. Good. I didn't want him to think I was beaten, because I wasn't. "My restaurant isn't for sale, if that's what you want to know."

He chuckled. How did he make a chuckle sound evil? I didn't know but he did. It could have been the circumstances under which the chuckle took place, since we were tied up and somewhat incapacitated. That lent itself to a certain level of evil.

Also, from what I could tell, this looked a lot like a lair. Maybe I'd watched too many movies. What-ever, it resulted in the same thing: this man was not on my side.

"I'm not interested in buying it," he said. "If I wanted a restaurant, I would have bought Solomon's after his untimely death."

"Friend of yours?" I asked.

"You might say that," he agreed.

Getzoff looked over at me, confused. "What the hell is going on here?"

I exhaled softly. "This man is a predator. I've been hunting him for years. He and six others raped and murdered my sister." After a beat, I added, "Five of those six are dead."

Getzoff shook his head and struggled against his bindings. "If you're trying to say…"

"That's exactly what she's trying to say," Hypnos said easily, like he was talking about what color marshmallow he preferred. "She murdered them. In cold blood."

I snorted softly. "There was nothing cold about it. I prefer to think of it as retribution for what they did to her. They had it coming."

"And you believe I have it coming," Hypnos said. "So you used this man to flush me out?"

"It worked, didn't it?" I asked. "Here you are, flushed like a piece of shit."

I cried out when he kicked me in the ribs.

"Bitch," he snarled. "You know nothing."

"I don't understand," Getzoff said.

"Allow me to illuminate you." The click of a switch sounded. The room was lit by a single bulb hanging from the ceiling.

Getzoff and I both stared.

"You." Getzoff looked confused.

"Me," Hypnos agreed. He was the man who sat beside Getzoff at dinner. The man he'd had a cordial conversation with. He'd walked right into my restaurant, sat down and ate, then drugged us.

"Who are you?" I asked.

Hypnos lowered himself back into the chair. "Allow me to introduce myself. My name is Harrison Frankel. Solomon was my cousin."

I should have seen that. The resemblance between them was clear, now I knew to look.

"My cousin and I didn't always get along, but I object to people killing him," Hypnos said.

"I don't know anything about that," I lied.

He gave me a droll look, clearly not believing a word.

"Solomon assaulted your sister. Killed her," he said slowly. "He went quiet for a while. Then he turned up dead. The next thing I knew, you bought his restaurant. Do you think I don't know what's going on under my nose?" He tapped the side of his. "Next thing I know someone is trying to find me. You might believe you're subtle, but you're anything but."

"And yet you took the bait," I said, offering a faint, insincere smile. "Otherwise I wouldn't be here."

Where was *here?* We seemed to be in some sort of industrial cannery, judging by the massive vat in the side of the room. It could fit about ten people standing side by side. Full of water, it would cover their heads. A ladder led up to the top of it, and set of stairs led out of the room. I guessed we were under-ground somewhere.

"You might want to arrest this man," I said.

Hypnos snorted. "He's in no position to arrest anyone. He's only here as a witness to your crimes. He had nothing to do with this. If it wasn't for you, he'd be tucked up in his bed, comfortable and alive."

"But he's—" I started to say.

Hypnos rose from his chair, pulled out a gun and put a bullet in the middle of Getzoff's head.

The shot rang out, echoing through the space so loud I was going to hear it for days.

"Do you see the blood trickling? Hypnos whispered. If he wasn't an evil asshole, his voice might sound hypnotic. "You did that to him."

He walked over to me and pulled out a knife.

I shrank away, but he put a hand on my shoulder and sliced through the zip tie that bound my hands. Gripping my wrist, he dragged me across the floor. He dumped me beside Getzoff and pressed my hand into the blood that was pooling on the concrete.

"Feel the blood you have on your hands," he said. "Figurative and literal. His death is your fault."

Getzoff"s blood was warm and sticky. The tang filling my nostrils.

I've smelled blood plenty of times before, but this time it made my stomach turn. I wanted to throw up everything I'd eaten for the last twenty-four hours.

Preferably on Hypnos' leather shoes.

I swallowed down the urge. I was tougher than this.

I jerked my wrist away from Hypnos. "What do you want?"

"I want you to stop hunting me and my associates," he said like nothing was simpler. Like they deserved to continue living their lives, when my sister couldn't.

"The only way I can ensure that is if you're dead." I closed my eyes, sure he was about to stab me or shoot me. I could try to run, but I wouldn't get far with my ankles tied together.

"Same with you," he said. Slowly, he tapped his long fingers against his thigh.

I forced my eyes open and locked my gaze on his. Maybe I could buy myself a little while longer.

"That doesn't work for me," I said evenly. "I have two restaurants to run. I'm a very busy woman, you know. This has been fun and all, but, it's time I left. Sorry to be a buzzkill for your little party." I shrugged one shoulder.

He chuckled. There it was again, that evil chuckle.

"I've never been a fan of the Irish exit," he said.

"I'm not Irish." I snuck out of plenty of parties though. None I wanted to leave more than this.

He stepped closer and put the knife away, somewhere under his leather jacket.

"You're not leaving either. No, I'm going to have a bit of fun with you first."

A chill went through me. I'd always considered the possibility they might use me like they did my sister, but I'd never been faced with it before. Bile threatened to rise again. His shoes were closer now. If I could aim just right…

He must have seen the expression on my face because he actually smiled.

"I'm not going to touch you. Not like that. You're far too tainted." He curled his lip in disgust.

One step toward me and the front of his left shoe would be right there, in front of my nose.

"In fact," he continued, oblivious to the peril the expensive leather was in, "before you die, you should be cleansed." He leaned over, grabbed me by the ankle and started to drag me across the floor, leaving a smear of Getzoff's blood behind me.

The concrete scraped my skin as I went, scrabbling for something to hold onto.

There was nothing.

All I could do was let myself be dragged over to the ladder that led up to the top of the enormous vat.

"It might be a little cold at first, but don't worry, it heats up quickly," he said.

I tried to wriggle away, but he grabbed me, hauling me up onto his shoulder.

I felt him grab hold of the ladder and start to climb. I kicked, struggling to throw myself out of his arms and back onto the hard floor.

He put an arm over me, holding me in place on his broad shoulders. His grip tight until we reached the top of the ladder.

"Say goodbye," he said.

He leaned over the vat and shoved me off him.

I let out a cry as I landed in the water with a splash.

# CHAPTER 22
## ARCHER

"I'm going to fucking kill whoever did this to us," I said.

"No, you're not." Boner was still shaking out his own arms and legs. "I'm going to kill them before you get there."

"Get in line," I told him.

"I am in line," he said, pushing himself to his feet. "I'm in line in front of you."

He squinted around. "She might be in the kitchen."

"She's not in there," Cass said, stepping out of the kitchen. "I'll check the storeroom."

He disappeared again, only to return half a minute later, shaking his head angrily.

"She's not there either."

I'd already come to that conclusion, but he had to check, just in case. She could have been lying somewhere hurt, just within reach.

"Our old mate Getzoff isn't here either," Boner said, straightening his hair.

"Do you think he took her?" Cass asked. He tangled his fingers in his fringe, tugging at it like it was the enemy.

"Someone fucking did," Jules snapped.

"Did you see who?" Boner asked. "You were outside."

No one missed the accusing tone in his voice, especially Jules, who took a step toward him.

"I was keeping a close eye on the place. The only people who came out were customers. Do you think I wouldn't notice someone carrying Harlow away? Assuming they carried her away." Now his expression was accusing.

Boner closed the distance between them until their chests were almost touching.

"What the hell are you saying?" he snarled. "That she drugged us and snuck out the door with Detective Getzoff?"

Jules opened his mouth to respond, but closed it again. The exhale he let out was ragged with barely contained frustration. Not at Boner for once. He cared about her as much as we did. I saw that on his face. This might be the first time he let himself admit it, even a little bit.

"She wouldn't do that," Cass said.

His faith in her was as unwavering as mine. Not to mention, if she wanted to poison us and walk out, she had plenty of opportunities to do it in the privacy of my apartment. She wouldn't taint Angel's Rest by doing it here. This was far too public.

And yet private enough for whoever actually put us out.

Assholes.

"They must have gone out the back," I concluded.

I rolled over and forced myself to my feet like a baby deer, even though my head was still groggy and aching.

I staggered a couple of steps before regaining my balance and walking to the back door. To the surprise of absolutely no one, it was unlocked.

Mindful there might be an ambush straight outside, I eased the door open.

"What are you doing?" Boner reached past me and shoved it the rest of the way.

"It's called being stealthy," I told him. "I thought you knew how to do that."

"I do know," he agreed. "But if they were going to

kill us, they would have done it while we were having a nap on the fucking floor, wouldn't they?"

"Only if they're thinking logically," I said. "This might come as a surprise to you, but not everyone does."

He looked like he was ready to argue, but his shoulders slumped.

"Yeah, I guess so." He perked up again a moment later. "After you then." He gestured toward the alley.

"Thanks. I think." I gave him the side eye before stepping past him and looking one way down the alley then the other.

As I expected, there was no sign of anyone.

I have to admit, I'd half-expected to find Harlow lying dead in the alley, her throat sliced. Or strangled, her eyes staring up at us. Lifeless. Her body already starting to cool. Possibly missing her heart.

If that happened, I'd be missing mine.

"Nothing here," I said over my shoulder.

I walked a few steps, my gaze scanning the ground. Nothing caught my eye. No cigarettes still cooling in the gutter. No accidentally abandoned identification that would lead us to whoever took her.

She was just…gone.

"So we know the culprit is one of four people," Boner said slowly. "We've already ruled out Harlow walking out and leaving. That narrows it down to three: Getzoff, Hypnos, and Zeus."

"We don't know Getzoff isn't one of them," Cass pointed out.

"Yes, we do," I said. "He was drugged too. He lost consciousness before the rest of us."

"Have you ever heard of a red herring?" Boner asked.

I scrubbed a hand over my face. "This isn't a mystery novel. Miss Marple isn't going to jump out and help us to solve this."

"I always preferred Sherlock Holmes," Boner said.

"He's not coming either," I pointed out.

"Not even Benedict Cumberbatch?" He looked disappointed.

"Not even him," I sighed. I wasn't sure what use an actor would be, if I'm honest. Although I was a big fan of his. I mean, his performance in *Doctor Strange*, am I right?

Anyway…

"We have to find her," Cass said. He pulled out his phone.

"What are you going to do? Post about her on social media?" Boner asked.

Cass glanced up at him before looking back at his phone screen.

"I'm going to track her phone."

"Oh," Boner said, with a nod. "That's a much better idea. Do that."

"I will," Cass said without looking up again. He tapped at his screen. His brow deeply creased as he worked.

"You're assuming her phone is still active," Jules said.

"What else have we got?" Cass didn't look up at him either. "I've got her. She's two blocks away. In that direction." He pointed south, before tapping at his screen again.

"What are you doing now?" Boner asked.

"Calling us an Uber," Cass explained. "It'll be quicker to drive two blocks than it will to run."

"Right," Boner said. "As long as we don't hit too many one-way streets." He scratched the side of his head. "I'm starting to think whatever they drugged us with has addled my brain."

"It came that way," Jules muttered.

"You might be right," Boner said cheerfully. He strode out to the street as the Uber pulled up.

"Can you tell us exactly where?" I asked.

"Right now I can," Cass said, "as long as her phone keeps…" He froze.

"What is it" Jules asked, all but shoving him into the waiting vehicle.

"It stopped." Cass looked devastated. "I don't

know why, but it stopped." His eyes shone in the light of a vehicle, traveling the other way, fear etched on his face. "What do we do?"

"What we were going to do anyway," Boner said reasonably. "We go there and we find her."

Cass nodded and sat with his elbows on his thighs. So far forward in his seat, I thought he might hit his head on the one in front of him. He, Boner and I huddled in the back, while Jules sat beside the driver in the front passenger seat.

None of us said a word while we travelled the two blocks, and climbed out of the Uber.

"This looks—" Cass started, staring at the building we stood in front of.

"Ordinary as fuck?" Boner offered.

"Yeah." Cass nodded. "An ordinary apartment building."

"I don't care what it is if she's in there," I said. "If we have to break down every single door to look inside, that's what we're going to do. Unless her phone is on again?"

Cass shook his head. "It's not. I have no idea which floor she was on. All I have is that she's in this building somewhere and she needs us."

Boner opened his mouth as if he was going to say something facetious. Like, 'The blip of her phone told you that?' For once, he closed it without speaking.

Now wasn't the time to be snarking at each other. Now was the time we had to work together to find our woman.

I pulled out my own phone and looked up the address.

"What are you doing?" Jules asked.

"I'm seeing if I can find a floor plan for this place," I said. "It'll be easier to figure out where to go if we have a map."

"Right," he said slowly. "Good idea."

I glanced over at him and gave him a faint upward twitch of my lips.

"Curious," I said, squinting at the screen to make sure I was seeing what I thought I was seeing.

"What's curious?" Boner asked, looking over my shoulder.

"Apparently this place is owned by Danforth Holdings."

"Danforth, as in Solomon Danforth?" Cass asked.

"Exactly," I said. Now we were both searching, our fingers flying over our screens.

"Solomon Danforth has a cousin named Harrison Frankel," Cass said. "He was out of the country until yesterday."

"Of course he fucking was," Boner said. "How much do you want to bet this asshole is Hypnos?"

"Nothing," I said, "because it makes too much sense."

"How does any of this help us find Harlow?" Jules demanded.

"It confirms the fact this building is suspicious as fuck," I said. "It has ten floors, two apartments per floor. And a basement."

"If I was going to do devious shit, I'd do it in the basement," Boner said.

I looked up at him, right in his eyes, and said, "So would I."

"How do we get into the basement?" Jules asked, taking a step toward the building.

I pinched the screen to take a closer look at the floor plan.

"There's a set of stairs off the main foyer. It leads to a door at the back of the building."

"Then that's where we go," Boner said. "By the way, I brought a little something with us."

From under his leather jacket he pulled a towel, one from Harlow's restaurant. The Angel's Rest logo was embroidered on the corner.

Holding it carefully he spread the sides out, one then the other, revealing five of her chef knives, shining in the streetlight.

I knew for a fact each one was wickedly sharp, ready to slice anything and anyone. I'd seen her use them with skill and dexterity, slicing everything like the knife was passing through butter.

They were perfect. Like her.

"I figured we should be prepared when dealing with Hypnos."

He offered us each a knife before taking one himself. "Let's go get this asshole."

# CHAPTER 23

## HARLOW

hit the base of the vat and kicked my legs to push myself back to the surface. The water was icy, a thousand tiny needles against my skin. Each one reminded me I was alive. While I was still breathing, I was going to keep fighting.

I popped out, gasping for air.

*Don't panic,* I told myself. *Think. You can do this.*

I had to.

I glanced up. The lip of the vat was too high to reach, even if I lunged. I pressed my palms against the sides and bobbed. Water dripped down my face, and my clothes were heavy, clinging to me everywhere, threatening to drag me back under.

"Like I said, it'll be a little cold at first," Hypnos' voice carried over the side of the vat. "In half an hour or so, it'll be at one hundred degrees. It'll keep climbing slowly until it reaches boiling point."

That *really* wasn't going to work for me. I didn't have 'be boiled alive' on my bingo card for this year. Or any other foreseeable year for that matter.

"You're not very nice," I called out.

He chuckled. "I've been told that before. The thing is, I don't care about being nice."

"You care about staying out of prison," I said.

"Yes, that is high on my list of priorities," he agreed.

"Making me into soup won't help you," I told him.

"It'll help me," he said. "I'll be getting rid of a menace. My associate will be pleased at my initiative."

"Are you sure about that?" I asked. "If Zeus is the big bad everyone is making him out to be, he might not care. He didn't seem particularly impressed with any of the rest of you. Why would you be any different?"

Something clattered against the side of the vat, followed by what sounded like him climbing up the ladder. His head appeared over the top, peering down at me.

"The others were different," he said. "They were lackeys. I'm Zeus's right-hand man."

"So you're the head lackey, I said. "I mean, right-hand man isn't the boss, is it?"

"Not yet," he agreed. "Until I take care of Zeus."

Hmm, interesting.

"So, in a manner of speaking, we're on the same side," I said. "We both want him taken care of. How about you let me out of here, and we can work together? Or better yet, you can tell me who he is, and I'll take care of him for you."

After I killed the hell out of Hypnos.

He snorted. "I wasn't born yesterday, Miss St. James. Nor do I need your help. When the time comes, I will deal with him."

"Okay, but can you satisfy my curiosity at least, since I'm about to be boiled alive?" I said. "Can you tell me who he is? I mean, what do you have to lose, right? You tell me, I die, the secret goes with me to…" I glanced down at the water. "I'm not going to get an actual grave, am I?"

"Probably not," he said. "I'll drain what's left out into the sewer."

I was tempted to remind him he wasn't nice, but I didn't think he'd forgotten since the last time I said it.

"Okay, I suppose it doesn't matter since I'll be dead anyway," I said. "So, who is Zeus? And how did you get into my kitchen to drug us?"

Hypnos considered for a moment. "Since you're going to die anyway…"

My eyes widened when he told me. I shouldn't have been surprised. Of course it would be someone that powerful and influential. Someone virtually untouchable.

When I got out of here, he was dead meat. I might even make him into a celebratory bowl of meatballs. Then take him to the park and feed him to the pigeons. They could shit him out all over the benches. That seemed like a fitting end for him.

As for who drugged us? That left me cold.

"Since I can't get out anyway, do you think you could pass me down something to cut the zip tie on my ankles?" I asked. That didn't seem like too much to ask. "It won't be any fun for you if I drown before the water gets to boiling point."

"That's very true," he drawled.

I grimaced to myself. A thing could either be true or not. It didn't need to be qualified with 'very' in front of it.

Yeah, I focus on niggling things at the wrong times. So sue me.

He disappeared, returning a minute or two later with a pair of scissors.

"Catch," he tossed them down to me. He watched

until I caught them, then jumped off the ladder, his footsteps moving away.

I caught them and turned around, pressing my back against the slowly warming vat. I raised my sopping legs and sniped off the zip tie.

There, that was a little better.

"Thanks," I called out over my shoulder.

"It's the least I could do to prolong my amusement," he said.

Of course that was why he did it. Sadistic bastard.

I slipped the scissors into my pocket and kicked my way over to the opposite side of the vat.

I felt along the side, searching carefully in the dim light. I almost missed it, almost swiped my hand along the steel too quickly. But I found it.

Grooves in the side of the vat. An escape route for anyone who fell in accidentally.

I sent a quick thanks for the OSHA people who gave a thought for the health and safety of workers. A safety feature like this would be a relatively recent addition, making me wonder how long this vat was down here.

"Is the water feeling more pleasant now? Hypnos asked.

"It's actually quite nice," I said. It was almost as warm as bath water. "I don't suppose you can throw in some bubble bath? Maybe a rubber duck?"

He laughed. "Those would be wasted in there."

"That's what I thought you'd say." I glanced back to make sure he hadn't climbed back up the ladder before working my hands and feet into the grooves and climbing slowly.

Dripping, I reached the top of the vat and grabbed the lip, pulling myself over as quickly as I could and dropping to the floor.

I winced, hoping like hell he didn't hear the wet plop as I landed.

I dropped to a crouch and waited.

"It should be getting nice and warm by now," he called out. "I'm sorry it won't warm up any faster."

I stood quickly so I could project my voice. Hopefully I sounded like I was still inside the enormous vat. "That's okay. I'm not in a hurry."

There was that evil chuckle again. "Of course you're not."

I pulled the scissors out of my pocket and stepped slowly around the vat, moving toward his voice, keeping my eyes and ears open.

After a step or two, I stopped to push off my footwear. Bare feet would be quieter than slopping along in my work shoes and socks. My shoes were probably ruined at this point anyway. If I wasn't already angry, I'd be angry over that. Those were a perfectly good pair of comfortable, worn in shoes.

I came around the side of the vat to see him sitting in the rickety chair he'd been in when I regained consciousness. He was bent over his phone, intent on something on the screen.

*Young people and their technology*, I thought to myself.

He was older than me and I was grateful for the distraction. Now, if it kept him busy for just long enough…

Silently, I moved toward him, hands wrapped around the finger loops of the scissors. Blades pointed in his direction.

One step.

Two steps.

Three steps.

I rushed at him but he turned around at the last moment and threw himself to his feet.

I lunged, but he grabbed my wrist, holding it right before I could plunge the scissors into his throat.

"Now, now, Miss St. James, is that any way to treat your host?" He clicked his tongue.

Since the answer was a definite yes, I raised my knee and jammed it into his groin.

He let out a muffled cry and let go of my wrist, dropping his hands to cover his delicate, and apparently painful, junk.

I drew my arm back and jammed the scissors into his jugular with everything I had. It was too blunt to slide in nicely. I had to force it in, pushing and shoving until it was nice and deep, blood squirting out and coating my fingers.

"Harlow!"

That was Cass' voice, calling out my name as he hurtled down the stairs so fast he almost lost his footing and face planted on the concrete floor.

Boner grabbed him at the last minute, holding him up while they both stepped off the stairs. Archer and Jules were right behind.

"You're just in time," I told them. "I was just dealing with our friend Hypnos here."

"Can we help?" Boner held up one of my kitchen knives.

"I guess he could use a few more holes." I yanked back the scissors.

Hypnos' eyes widened. He clutched at his throat, desperately trying to stem the flow of blood.

Grinning, Boner stepped up behind him and drove the knife into his back, not enough to kill him quicker, but enough to hurt like a motherfucker.

Archer was right beside him, doing the same thing on the opposite side of his back.

Cass closed his eyes and turned his face before, poking his knife roughly in the direction of Hypnos' ribs. He made a face as it scraped against bone, the sound audible throughout the basement.

Grimacing, he dropped the knife and shook his hand.

"Good job," Boner told him, patting him on the shoulder.

"Yeah." Cass looked like he might be sick.

Hypnos started to crumple, falling to the floor with the two knives sticking out of him. He landed with a thunk. Writhed a few times before lying still.

Jules shrugged and leaned over to stab his knife into Hypnos' left ass cheek. It wobbled back and forth when he let it go.

He straightened up and stood back. "I figured I should get in on the fun."

"I wish I thought of that," Boner said, looking at him appreciatively.

"You're already a pain in the ass," Jules told him, but he was actually smiling.

Boner grinned back and flipped him off with both middle fingers. "Love you too, bro."

"So, this was Hypnos?" Archer asked.

"Another name off my list." I rubbed the tattoos on my arm.

Six down, one to go. I already had a head start on Zeus. I knew who he was. The question was, what was I going to do with that information?

My men, they came after me. Found me here. That didn't mean I could trust them.

After what Hypnos told me about how we were drugged, I wasn't sure I could trust anyone.

How had they found me so quickly? I didn't want to think any of these things, but Hypnos put the doubt in my mind, and right now it was starting to fester.

"Are you okay?" Cass put his arms around me.

In spite of my misgivings, I melted into his arms.

"I'm okay," I said. "A little bit wet and cold, but alive."

I was starting to shiver. The cold of the air had worked its way under my wet clothes, under my skin and into my bones.

"Let's get you out of here and into a nice hot bath," Boner said.

"As long as it's not as big as that." I jerked my head toward the vat, which was starting to steam. Much longer in there, and I would have been chef soup.

"What are we going to do with Hypnos?" Cass asked. He looked like he hoped it wasn't anything gory.

"We're going to leave him right where he is," Boner said. "Full of those chef knives."

"That's why you brought them." Archer asked. He seemed impressed.

Boner shrugged a shoulder modestly. "I thought we might need them, but I also figured this was a good way for Chef Stabby to finally get recognized."

"I didn't use any of those on him," I pointed out.

Boner grinned and scooped up the knife Cass dropped, offering it to me hilt first. He waggled his eyebrows at me and stepped back.

I contemplated for a moment before deciding he'd look weird if I didn't do this. I crouched down and drove the blade into his other ass cheek. He had two in his back and two in his butt.

Perfectly balanced.

"Let's get out of here." Cass took my hand and led me toward the stairs and out of the basement.

I stopped halfway up to glance back, making sure Hypnos was dead.

Satisfied he wasn't moving or breathing, I followed the guys out.

# CHAPTER 24

## HARLOW

I sat with my elbows on the table, hands wrapped around my mug. My guys were talking but I didn't hear what they were saying. A word here or there filtered into my brain, but that was all. Mostly, I was lost in my thoughts.

Boner slapped something down on the table in front of me and said, "Penny for them." He lifted his hand to reveal what looked like a newly minted penny. Pennies aren't even being made anymore.

"Where did you get that?" I picked it up and turned it around in my fingers.

"Never mind where I got it," he said. He pulled out the chair beside me and sat, perched on the edge, leaning toward me. "What's going on in that beautiful head of yours?" His blue eyes were troubled. Worried for me.

"It was a long night," I started. I managed a couple of restless hours of sleep before I had to get back up and get ready for work.

"It was, but we're here for you. You know that, right?"

"Of course I do," I said quickly. Maybe a little too quickly.

He took the penny from my fingers and laced his hand in mine. "I'm sorry for what happened to you. I wish I figured out what was going down sooner, like, before we were drugged, not after." The regretful expression on his face suggested he'd be beating himself up about that for a long time to come.

"Yeah." I averted my gaze.

"What?" he asked, leaning in closer. "It wasn't you, was it?"

My gaze snapped back to his. "Of course not. Do you really think I'd drug myself?"

"No, I don't," he said. "But something is going on with you and I want to know what it is. How are we supposed to help you if you won't open up to us?"

He was right. I knew that, but Hypnos's words kept going around and around in my brain like a song on repeat. The kind of song you wish you never heard in the first place. The kind that stuck in your mind for days after, until you wished some other earworm would come along.

"Did Hypnos tell you who drugged us?" Cass stood behind Boner, a hand on his shoulder. The pair seemed to be getting closer. I loved that for them.

"Whatever he said, he's full of shit," Jules said. He was leaning against the fridge, his arms crossed like he was guarding the food. I didn't know why and from who. None of us seem to have much of an appetite.

"Maybe he was," I said, only offering him a glance, before looking back to Boner. "Maybe he wasn't."

Jules pushed himself away from the fridge and stepped closer to the table. "What are you saying?"

"Boner came into the kitchen while you weren't there," Cass said, looking down at him like he couldn't believe he was saying those words.

"What the fuck?" Boner looked over his shoulder. "I was making sure you were okay. Do you think I slipped something into the food?" He looked back at me in disbelief. "Is that what that prick told you? That I did this? Do you think I'm working with him? I didn't know who he was until last night."

"People don't always know who they're working for," Jules pointed out. "If someone contacts you indirectly, you can—"

Boner shoved himself to his feet. "You can fuck

right off with that bullshit. I wasn't working with Hypnos. I wasn't working with anyone but the people in this room. I can't believe you'd accuse me of this."

He hesitated for a moment before pointing at Jules. "Okay, you I can believe. Not the rest of you." He flicked his finger around the room.

"No one's accusing you," I said. "Hypnos didn't say anything about you."

Boner stared at me for a moment, my words slowly sinking in before he sank back into his chair.

"Of course he didn't. I have nothing to do with what happened. If I find them, I mean *when* I find them, I'm going to stab them in the ass too." He nodded to punctuate the threat.

I managed a faint smile.

"Whatever he said, it put you on edge," Cass said, coming around to stand behind me and massage my shoulders.

I tried not to flinch.

"He did try to boil me alive," I pointed out. That would rattle the hell out of anyone. Last night was the closest I ever came to dying. I didn't want to repeat the experience anytime soon.

"Yeah, he did. But you're holding back on us," Cass insisted. If he was going to use his dominant tone to force the words out of me. I was going to be in trouble.

"I think I speak for everyone here when I say we're not letting you out of here until you tell us what he said." Jules moved a couple of steps to stand in front of the door, like he was now guarding the only way out.

He wasn't. If I wanted to, I could make a run for it and be out the fire escape before he could move.

I didn't. I closed my eyes and drew in a long breath through my nose and out again.

"It was gas," I said. "They left a canister that put us all to sleep."

"So they only gassed the people who were left at the end of the night," Archer reasoned. "How did they know we'd be staying?"

"Because Hypnos was right there watching," I said. "He saw me offer the coffee to Detective Getzoff. He knew we were staying, so he came back with a couple of his minions. They tied all of you up while Hypnos took me and Getzoff."

"What canister? Where?" Jules asked, abandoning his post at the door to step over closer. His eyes were half closed like he was turning thoughts around and around in his mind.

"That's a surprisingly good question," Boner said.

"Thanks," Jules said sarcastically.

"You're welcome," Boner, said, as if he missed the sarcasm altogether. "How *did* the gas get there?"

"It was left under the table by one of my staff. All Hypnos had to do was pretend to adjust his shoe. He opened it under the tablecloth and left."

"What a sneaky bastard," Boner said. "I thought he looked sus as fuck when he walked through the door."

"You could have said something," Cass told him.

Boner shrugged. "Who am I to point fingers at other people? Believe it or not, some people might suggest I'm sus as fuck."

No one took that bait.

"It's true what they say," Archer said. "It really is hard to find good help."

I snorted softly.

"Which one of them was it?" Cass asked, leaning down to press my cheek to his. "For the record, it wasn't me."

"Of course it wasn't," Jules said. He glanced around at all of us as if daring us to contradict him.

We didn't. We all knew where Cass' loyalties lay, and it wasn't with someone like Hypnos.

"I don't know who it was," I admitted. "It could be Yvette or Shelly. Maybe both. I have no idea. Hypnos wasn't forthcoming with specifics."

I wanted to stab him again for not being clearer.

I'd asked, but he told me it didn't matter, since I'd never see my restaurants again.

"Now that's a mindfuck," Boner said. "If we accuse one, we could accuse the wrong one. If we kill them both, we could be killing someone who's innocent. If you don't, and they're both guilty…"

He didn't need to finish that. If they were working against us, we couldn't leave them alive. How would we know which one it was though? Was it one, or both of them?

We couldn't fling accusations around, not when it was possible one of them hadn't done anything at all. Enough innocent blood had been spilled already.

"It turns out Getzoff wasn't working with Hypnos," I said with a sigh. "He really was trying to find a serial killer."

"He found a few of them," Boner said cheerfully.

"It didn't do him much good," I said. "He still ended up dead." I curled and uncurled my hands, but I swear I could still feel his blood coating my fingers.

I used him as bait and he'd paid the price. And what for? Hypnos would have come after me anyway. He knew who I was. Chances were, so did Zeus. He could be planning something as we sat here talking.

We were going to have to go after him and quickly.

"You can't open Angel's Rest today," Cass said firmly. "Not when one of your staff might have betrayed you."

"Yes, you should." Boner started smiling slowly. "I have an idea."

# CHAPTER 25

## HARLOW

"I don't know about this," I said, trying to focus on making ravioli. Shame there were no bits of Hypnos in it.

"It'll be fine, trust me," Boner said. "Take a deep breath. You know what you have to do."

"Right." I fed more pasta through the pasta machine, flattening it out into a long sheet.

A message pinged on Cass' phone. He pulled it out of his pocket and glanced at it.

"Jules said they're both heading this way."

I swallowed hard.

"They have some balls, I have to give them that," Boner said. "Or what is it? Cast iron ovaries?"

I managed a short, nervous laugh. "One or the other." I knew Shelly had the first, but that was none of my business.

"Play it cool," he said as the back door opened and someone stepped inside.

I turned in time to see Shelly, her bag over her shoulder.

"Morning, Chef," she called out cheerfully.

"Morning," I replied as if nothing was amiss.

"Everyone seemed to have fun last night," she said, stopping by the kitchen door.

Fun? That was one word for it. I'd almost forgotten we had the dinner the night before.

"Yeah, we should do it again sometime," I said.

With a different ending next time.

She grinned. "I'm here for it. They were all tipping like they'd never tipped before."

"That's great," I said sincerely. If that was the case, and she was innocent, I'd happily hold another dinner. Once Zeus was dead.

She headed off to the office to put down her things and fix her uniform.

"One down, one to go," Archer said softly.

I hummed my agreement. What was I going to do if Yvette seemed just as innocent?

I stepped away from the pasta maker, over to the doorway as Yvette stepped through.

She looked surprised to see me. Her face paled. She turned to run.

"Bingo," Boner called out.

We all bolted after her.

I was barely out the back door when she ran into Jules as he stepped into the alley. He grabbed hold of her, whipped her around and held her arms behind her back.

"Looks like we have ourselves a guilty party," Boner said, stepping over to her.

She lifted her chin in defiance. "I don't know what you're talking about."

"Innocent people don't run off like that," I pointed out. "You look like you saw a ghost."

She curled her lip at me before she could stop herself.

"Why did you do it?" I asked.

"I know who you are," she said, making no effort to keep her voice down. "You're a murderer." She spat in the direction of my shoes.

Lucky she missed. These were my only spare pair.

"Harlow could have died." Jules twisted her arms a little more.

She bit back a cry of pain. "That was the idea."

"Why?" Cass demanded. "Why would you want her dead?"

"Because she wanted to kill my father," Yvette snarled.

I stared at her for a moment.

"Hypnos was your father."

She had the same eyes as him. The same hair color. Different enough that I didn't pick on the resemblance until now. Seeing her in front of me? It should have been obvious.

It took a moment for my words to sink in. When they did, she sagged. Just a little, because Jules held her upright.

"Was?" she whispered.

"You haven't heard?" Boner asked happily. "He had an unfortunate run-in with some sharp objects. After he tried to turn my woman into soup." His tone and expression became dangerous.

Her gaze snapped to him. "He wouldn't do that. He was trying to save himself from her. Because she's coming after him and people like him for no reason." She didn't look so sure.

"He was right, I was going after him," I said evenly. "But not for no reason."

In as few words as possible, because we were standing in public, I explained why I'd hunted them down. Why I'd killed them.

By the time I was finished, tears trickled down her cheeks.

"He wouldn't do that," she whispered again.

"He did do that," Jules snapped.

She whimpered. "I'm sorry, I had no idea. If I did, I would have—"

Jules must have loosened his grip, because she jerked herself away and turned around to take a swing at him. He caught her fist with his hand right before it hit him in the jaw.

"Not this time," he said. The last time anyone tried to punch him, he ended up with some impressive bruises. "What are we going to do with her?"

I considered for a moment. If we let her go, she could well run off to Zeus. If we didn't, it meant killing her. I didn't like killing women, but what choice did I have?

"Ravioli," Boner suggested.

"You wouldn't." Yvette tried to jerk away from Jules, but his grip on her hand was too tight.

"Yeah, we would," Boner said, grinning.

"No we won't," I said finally. "We're going to have to put her away somewhere while we deal with Zeus."

She hadn't harmed me, but she was complicit. Part of me wanted to let her go, but I didn't dare. If I turned my back on her, she might drive a knife into it. That was a risk I couldn't take, not with myself and not with any of my men either. Archer would have pointed out the saying, 'The apple doesn't fall far from the tree.' If that was the case here, we needed to treat her like her father treated me.

"I'm not going to do anything to you," Yvette said,

pleading. "Let me go and you never have to see me again." She blinked more tears out of her eyes.

"Unfortunately, I hold a grudge," I said. "You knew what he wanted to do with me, and you helped make it happen. That makes you the enemy in my book."

She sniffed. "Please, I promise I won't…"

I ignored her. "Jules, can you bring her inside?"

He nodded and started to let go of her hand.

She took that moment to jerk away from him and make a run for it. She darted toward the end of the alley and out onto the street, straight into the path of a yellow taxi.

Tires squealed. The driver tried to avoid her, but the vehicle slammed right into her, throwing her body up into the air before it came back down to the road with a crunch that made me wince.

"Or that could happen," Boner said.

"Yeah." That took care of that problem.

As if I was in a dream, I watched the driver climb out of the car and step over to check on her. I couldn't hear him but I read his lips when he mouthed, "She's dead."

"I guess I'm going to need to find a new server," I said with a sigh.

After I found Zeus and ended him.

# EPILOGUE
## ZEUS

*Chef Stabby,* I read with some amusement.

Harlow St. James was proving to be a bigger problem than I anticipated. Hypnos should have been able to take care of her. Last night was supposed to be the end of it. No more having to worry she'd sneak in here in the middle of the night and try to cut my throat. Not that she'd get past my security system.

"I'm going to have to take care of her myself," I said under my breath, "Enjoy your last few days on this earth, Chef St. James. They're just about to come to a sticky end."

# BONUS EPILOGUE
## HARLOW

Harlow

George Wentworth stared at me. He'd been doing that for the last hour, without blinking. It was starting to become disconcerting.

"You deserved it," I said to the corpse, who lay on the tiled floor, a knife protruding from his chest.

I sat beside him, my arms around my legs, my chin on my knees.

This wasn't the first time I killed someone, but it was the second. The same nausea I experienced after Fred Alonso's death chased me right now. So far, I held on to the contents of my stomach.

Remorse? There wasn't any. Why was I still sitting here while his body was getting cold? I should be getting the hell out of here.

I startled as the door creaked behind me.

I spun around as someone stepped inside. Dressed completely in black, they looked like a shadow, from their shoes, to the mask covering their face. They walked over to look down at Wentworth, shoulders sagging.

"Looks like I was too late."

He pulled off his mask with one hand and let it dangle from his fingers. He was undeniably attractive, with dark hair, dark eyes and a square jaw.

"Sorry, did you have dibs on this?" I asked.

I might as well make light of it. He caught me red-handed. Was he about to call the cops on me? Was I going to have to kill him too? I had five more predators to hunt down and remove. Two out of a list of seven wasn't enough.

He shrugged, the movement so small I almost missed it. "Not particularly. It's good to see him dead."

He tucked his spare hand into his pocket.

"Yeah." I glanced back at Wentworth.

His cold blue eyes were colder still in death. I didn't think too many people would mourn his loss. Me? I might go out for a celebratory drink after this.

"Do you need some help cleaning up?" the newcomer asked. "I'm Archer, by the way. Archer Hardwick."

It didn't seem that he was going to call the cops on me.

"Harlow St. James," I said, wondering if I was out of my mind to tell him who I was.

"Nice to meet you, Harlow." He leaned over to offer his hand.

I shook it and pushed myself to my feet. "I'd love some help. I haven't quite gotten the clean-up part down to a fine art yet."

The sides of his mouth twitched. "You will. I'll take his hands if you can grab his feet."

I nodded and did as he asked.

We picked up Wentworth and slowly moved across the room and out the door. Parked just outside was a vehicle. Archer's, I assumed.

I was sweating by the time we tossed Wentworth into the back.

Archer closed the door on his corpse grabbed out a couple of brushes and a bucket. He handed them to me, then got out a bottle of bleach.

"Always a good idea not to leave any evidence behind," he asked.

"Right, good idea."

We headed back inside, where he opened the bleach and tipped some onto the blood on the floor. We started to scrub, cleaning up every drop, before wiping it dry with a towel.

"There, no one will ever know we were here," he said, nodding at our work. He seemed satisfied with the job we'd done. Of course he was. We'd been meticulous, cleaning everywhere twice over.

"Thank you, I appreciate this," I said. I was going to have to get myself some bleach and scrubbing brushes.

"Anytime," Archer said. "Let's get rid of the rest of him."

He closed the door behind us and wiped the knob clean, making sure we didn't leave any evidence behind there either. He really was meticulous. A girl could learn a lot from him.

I should probably walk away right now, but when he gestured for me to sit in the passenger's seat, I found myself climbing inside.

"Make sure you fasten your seatbelt," he said. "They reduce the risk of death by about half if we have an accident."

"Right." I gave him a funny look before clicking mine in. Apparently he was as meticulous about safety as he was about cleaning. I shouldn't judge him. Those were important things to be meticulous about.

After a couple of blocks, we stopped at the side of the road, beside an alley. I squinted, but couldn't even see to the other side, it was too dark.

"This looks like a good place," he said. "He won't be found here for a while."

I couldn't argue with that. We'd be long gone before anyone came here.

I unfastened my seatbelt and followed him out of the car.

Looking around carefully to make sure no one was watching, because that definitely wouldn't be safe for us, he opened the back of the car. Between us, we managed to pull Wentworth out, his body still floppy. Eyes still staring accusingly.

*You should have thought of that before you laid a hand on my sister,* I told him silently. If I was being fair, he probably didn't think he would end up this way.

Both of us puffing lightly, we carried him over to a dumpster in the middle of the alley.

I hadn't seen it before in the darkness. I guessed this wasn't a first for Archer. That should be disturbing as fuck, but since he was helping me to cover a murder it was less disconcerting than it might have been.

I shouldn't admit this, but it was actually kind of hot.

"On three," Archer said. "One, two, three."

We swung Wentworth as Archer counted down, then heaved him into the dumpster. His body fell in with a satisfying thud. The kind that sounds final, so you know an ordeal has come to an end.

Or at least, this one long night.

Archer wiped his hands on his jeans and closed the dumpster.

"I wouldn't mind if the trash took itself out," he said. "But sometimes it needs a bit of help."

I laughed softly. "Yes, it does."

He regarded me for a moment. "Do you want to go for a coffee?"

"Sure," I said, as if it was the most normal thing in the world. "I'd like that."

I had a feeling I was going to be seeing more of Archer. "You didn't tell me why you were there to kill him," I said.

Did he have a grudge for a different reason than I did? As far as I knew, people didn't usually go around trying to murder people. I didn't; just *particular* people.

"I'll tell you over coffee," he said, closing the back of the car. "I'd like to hear your reasons."

"It's a long story," I said.

"That's okay." He slid back into the driver's seat and waited until I was in the passenger side before saying, "I have all night."

Thank you for reading! The story concludes in Heart Beating.

# ABOUT THE AUTHOR

Maggie Alabaster writes reverse harem and, paranormal, sci-fi and fantasy romance.

She lives in NSW, Australia with one spouse, two daughters, one dog, and countless birds.

Jo Bradley writes contemporary romance.

Sign up for Maggie's newsletter! Sign Up!

Join Maggie's reader group! Join here!

Follow Maggie on Bookbub! Click here to follow me!

Check out Maggie's website- www.maggieal abaster.com

# ALSO BY MAGGIE ALABASTER

Best Served Cold

Heart Stopping

Heart Rending

Heart Breaking

Heart Beating


Aurora Hollow duet

Take Me Slowly Part 1

Take Me Slowly Part 2


Ruck Boys

Filthy Ruck

Hard Ruck

Twisted Ruck

Bad Ruck

Dirty Ruck

Deadly Ruck


Sparrow and the Mafia Kings

Possessive

Ruined

Corrupted

Pucking Dark Hearts

Pucking Hearts Collide

Pucking Forbidden Hearts

Pucking Hardened Hearts

Dusk Bay Demons

Puck Drop

Breakaway

Power Play

Brutal Academy

Book 1 Heartless

Book 2 Cruel

Book 3 Vengeful

Court of Blood and Binding

Book 1 Song of Scent and Magic

Book 2 Crown of Mist and Heat

Book 3 Sword of Balm and Shadow

Book 4 Whisper of Frost and Flame

Dark Masque

Book 1 Bait

Book 2 Prey

Book 3 Trap

Novella A Very Dark Masque Christmas


Saving Abbie

Book 1 Pitch

Book 2 Pound

Book 3 Session

Book 4 Muse

Book 5 Rhythm

Book 6 Encore

Novella Venomous

Saving Abbie books 1-4

Saving Abbie books 4-6 + Venomous


Ruthless Claws

Book 1 Ivory

Book 2 Crimson

Book 3 Elodie


Harmony's Magic

Book 1 Summoned by Fire

Book 2 Summoned by Fate

Book 3 Summoned by Desire

Shifter's Vault

Book 1 Discarded

Book 2 Deceived

Book 3 Disgraced


My Alien Mates

Book 1 Star Warriors

Book 2 Star Defenders

Book 3 Star Protectors


Academy of Modern Magic

Book 1 Digital Magic

Book 2 Virtual Magic

Book 3 Logical Magic

Complete Collection


Summer's Harem

Book 1: Shimmer

Book 2: Glimmer

Book 3: Flicker

Complete collection


Short reads

Taken by the Snowmen

Jingle All the Way

Also by Maggie Alabaster and Erin Yoshikawa

Caught by the Tide

Book 1–Pursued by Shadows

Book 2 Pursued by Darkness

Book 3 Pursued by Monsters